THE FAIRIES WANT ME DEAD

A FAE DEFENCE SOCIETY NOVEL

MARK HOOD

UNSEELIE PRESS

UNSEELIE PRESS

ISBN: 1-913442-08-X
ISBN-13: 978-1-913442-08-8

Cover design by MiblArt
miblart.com

LEARN THE SECRETS OF THE FAE DEFENCE SOCIETY

Visit the website and sign up to receive a secret bundle of files revealing the work of the Fae Defence Society going on throughout history. This will also sign you up to our mailing list to keep you updated with the fight against the fae.

https://faedefencesociety.com/newsletter/
Stay watchful.

For Martyne, of course.

Contents

Chapter One

A Surprising Bequest

I finished sending the last of the emails on my phone, and stared out of the train window watching the scenery flash by. A mountain of paperwork sat on the table in front of me, where I'd signed it, photographed it and emailed it back to the solicitor.

"He understood, you know," she said.

"I'm sorry?" I said. The woman had joined the train at the last station and planted herself in the seat opposite mine with a waft of lavender. Until now, she'd sat in silence as I worked through the stack of legal documents.

"Your grandfather, dear," she said in a tone suggesting she thought I was slow on the uptake. I looked up and her bright green eyes locked with mine. "He wanted to keep you safe but that meant you needed to stay away."

I tried to ignore her, frowning at the view outside, but I found my gaze drawn back to meet her eyes. Her liver-spotted hands and the grey hair trying to escape a bun suggested she was the far side of 80, or even 90, but those eyes sparkled with youth.

"You had your own life, Richard. He was glad you did, in fact. He didn't want you to become like him at the end."

"I'm sorry, what are you talking about? How do you know my

name?"

Her eyes pierced me. I shifted in my seat as the silence grew longer. "No, you're not ready yet," she mumbled. She glanced past me out of the window, said "Oh, this is me," and stood. The train lurched with a hiss of hydraulics as we slowed into the station, and she grabbed my arm to steady herself. She turned back to me one last time, her head close to mine and her knotted fingers tight on my shoulder.

"Don't dig too deep," she urged me, in a low quiet voice. Then, in a brighter tone, she added "you have his eyes, you know."

With that she hurried off the train, faster than I'd have expected her to move. I scanned the crowd on the platform, craning my neck to see where she'd gone, but couldn't find her.

When I turned back, I saw the paperwork still spread across the table. She must have spotted the letters and decided to cheer up the sad-looking and distracted middle-aged man with a letter about a deceased relative. My wedding ring told her I had a family of my own, and she'd amused herself on a dull train journey.

A few minutes later, and with the help of a hot cup of coffee, my glum mood had broken. Reflecting that at least the old woman's trick had cheered me up, I sat and worked on the crossword.

The morning had dawned gloomy and damp. Even by mid-afternoon, mist still blanketed the streets as I slowly drove along the road searching for the house number. The street in Newcastle that my grandfather's house occupied was quiet and leafy, in a pleasant area on the outskirts of town, and in better weather it would be quite a pretty location. I had expected something grimmer, if I was honest. I pulled up outside number 19 and fingered the outline of the key through the envelope the lawyer had handed me.

The house was dark and musty, and the light switch inside the door did nothing. I stepped over the pile of junk mail on the mat and opened the curtains of each room as I explored.

Grandad had always lived simply since Grandma had died, and each room was as dull and undecorated as the last. Magnolia walls unadorned by photographs or artworks, worn carpets and plain white doors greeted me throughout. Only the living room showed any signs of personalisation, with a bookcase along one wall beside the armchair. I tried to ignore the photograph of myself and a pregnant Claire and focused on the books. My grandfather had worked as a book binder, and these were gorgeous examples of his handiwork. I smiled to remember reading from them, sitting on his lap as a child. I carried them to my rental car and loaded them into the back.

Upstairs proved equally bland, except for one locked room at the front of the house. I recalled that in checking the bedroom I'd seen a key on the bedside table, and it turned in the lock with a well-oiled click.

If the rest of the home was spartan, this room could not have been more cluttered. Floor-to-ceiling shelves bowed under the weight of books and papers. Most were obscured by boxes piled in front of them waist high. More books, old newspapers and scribbled notes buried a small desk, while to either side yet more boxes obscured the window. I picked a path through the clutter, causing a minor avalanche of documents over the desk.

Perhaps the deeds to the house were in here somewhere. I looked for a logical order to the boxes. Written on the side of them were confusing categories: 'Scandinavian', 'Guarding and Warding', 'Species Variety: Europe'. A box marked 'British Romantic Nonsense' drew my attention by its name and I pulled it towards me. File folders and newspaper and magazine cuttings filled it to bursting, two battered hardback books and a few mouldering photographs on top. One of the magazine articles caught my eye. Two young girls in Yorkshire in the 1920s claimed to play with fairies at the bottom of the garden and produced photographs as evidence. This article dated from the 1980s when one of them admitted she'd faked it. A small note paper-clipped to the back of the article read 'As expected! See JW 1921/01-D & seq. See also Doyle'.

He'd been researching fairies? I rooted through the box for more clippings. They went back decades and referred to fairies, elves and other fanciful things. No wonder he'd labelled it 'Romantic Nonsense', but why collect it at all? Perhaps he'd been writing a book? I preferred that to the thought of his going senile.

I opened another box labelled 'Middle-East/Near Asia' and this was full of articles on the occult too. I found fewer newspaper articles and photocopied pages, and more slips of paper from magazines. These dealt with myths and legends of the Arabian Peninsula, from djinns and genies to peculiar-sounding creatures that lived in sand dunes and preyed on unwary travellers. An envelope contained a microcassette from an old dictation machine or portable recorder. I remembered seeing a dictaphone on the desk, so I slotted the cassette into it and hit play. Nothing happened. I fiddled with it for a while before giving up and dropping it into my jacket pocket to pick up new batteries later.

I looked through the transcript. It was a tale told by a Bedouin of a creature called a *dzokhim* that had kidnapped his daughter. Odd as this sounded, most surprising was that my grandfather had done the interview himself. The date at the top read 1973. His involvement that long ago confirmed this was not a symptom of dementia. If he had been writing a book though, where was it? Those in the bookcase were all works on the unseen world which they claimed surrounded and penetrated our own. A few appeared to be critical, debunking the entire area of research as misguided. Others were more balanced pieces weighing up the 'evidence' for and against the paranormal. But the majority were credulous books by staunch believers, recounting each half-remembered glimpse of a movement in a field as a sign of fairy revellers. Nothing bore my grandfather's name, so I turned to the desk.

Everything on the desktop was a photocopy or clipping rather than written notes, but in the middle drawer I found a leather-bound ledger, slightly bigger than a phone book. There were no markings on the cover, no title or author information. The books Grandad had created always sported gold embossed lettering. Soft covers flopped in my hands as I cleared a space for it and unwound the thin leather strip that held it shut. The title page read:

A Practical Guide to Countering the Fae Threat
    Compiled by H. Williams Esq. from the records and communications of the Fae Defence Society.
    For the benefit of its members.

Howard Williams, that was him and this must be what he had been working on. I flicked through the book, all written in my grandfather's dense, neat handwriting. There were chapters such as 'Identification', 'Habitat', 'Protection', 'Magic'. This last was a list of spells and incantations to do various things such as 'Reveal That Which Is Hidden' or 'Send Back To Whence It Came That Most Evil'. I stopped at the chapter titled 'Field Reports' and read a page at random.

Chapter Two

A Curious Discovery

1897, January 14th: A learned member reports a sighting of a hob in a cottage in Berwick-Upon-Tweed.

J___ G_____, a member in good standing supplied the following information.

A gentleman of my acquaintance was complaining one evening of his wife's misapprehension that their home was haunted. All of his entreaties to the contrary had been rebuffed, and he feared that she was working herself into a hysteria. I agreed to accompany my friend home to reassure her likewise, as he believed that with my background in local mythology I would be better able to convince her of her foolishness. Secretly I hoped that the haunting would prove genuine, which would afford me an opportunity to investigate the phenomenon properly. As the fine gentlemen of the Society will know, my primary interest is in the barrier between worlds, and my belief that only those who have traversed it are able to offer us information. In this event I would perform a cleansing ritual to rid the house of the troublesome spectre, and this would have the happy circumstance of also reassuring the distraught housewife that something had been done. During our brief journey I asked questions of him as to the nature of the disturbances his wife believed to be caused by this spirit. By his responses, I quickly ascertained that, while he had himself witnessed some of the incidents in question, he was not of the opinion that they were inexplicable by normal means. In particular, when items were found to be missing from their accustomed place, he believed his wife had removed them for cleaning and then forgotten where she had left them. He suspected that as her belief in the haunting grew, so too did her disquiet; this distraction then led in turn to her absent-mindedness, which reinforced her belief that things were going missing. My friend seemed quite pleased with his reasoning, and I saw no reason to disabuse him of the notion.

Upon arrival, his wife did not seem at all hysterical, but calmly and politely welcomed me into her home and announced she would prepare a pot of tea. I informed her that her husband had invited me to verify his belief that there were no vexatious spirits in the home, but that I wished to examine the place before I made a pronouncement (having previously agreed with my friend that this would be a suitable ruse to reassure her). I thus excused myself and, while she laboured in the kitchen, I proceeded to check the building for spirit-signs. Finding none, I retrieved my hag-stone from my pocket and peering through it espied the telltale footprints of a hob, forming a path between the kitchen and the stairs. I followed where they led me, up to the small bedroom above. Surely enough, there was the nest tucked into the space between the bed-head and the wall. Only one creature was there, who cowered from me when he became aware that I knew of his presence. He was a small fellow for his type, no more than 3 inches, yet was fully grown. I dealt with him in the usual manner.

Upon my return downstairs, not failing to secrete the hag-stone before rejoining the two, I informed the wife that nothing was there to trouble her and that all would be well from this point onwards. My friend began to rail again upon the subject of her wild imaginings and near-hysterical beliefs, and I sorely believe that had I not been there she would have burst into floods of tears. Once his anger subsided at the sight of her upset, I requested of my friend whether he had located that certain copy of a book I had wished to read, which he had informed me he possessed, and he retired to retrieve it for me. I took advantage of his absence to inform his wife that she had not, in fact, imagined anything but that the troublesome sprite would no longer offend her. If she wished to ensure freedom from such visitations, it would not hurt to leave a small plate of scraps from the evening meal out upon her retiring to bed.

There were many more of these stories. I read a few others, which spanned the last century or more. Some were more vague, others more violent, but all were reports of strange creatures and activities. Similar tales filled out the rest of the chapter, but at least I now knew why he'd been collecting those reports over the years. I removed my glasses, closed my eyes and pinched at the bridge of my nose. It was a clever conceit for a book, I had to admit. A guide to the paranormal passed off as fact. I could see that in these times where every other TV show had zombies, vampires or other supernatural protagonists, a work of fiction purporting to be a defence against such beings should prove popular. It looked as if he had almost finished it too. Could I get it published? He'd put a great deal of work into it, and it felt only right to get what might well be his life's work recognised.

A soft chime from my phone surprised me — my wife Claire had sent me a text asking how it was going. I dashed off a quick reply to her, promising to call later, and realised it was getting dark.

I returned to my car with the book under my arm. As I got in, I saw a figure across the foggy street, dressed in a long black coat, staring at the house, at me. My heart in my mouth, I peered closer and realised I was glaring at a large black dustbin. I laughed at my skittishness, understanding better how people would believe they'd seen fairies at the bottom of the garden.

As I drove away, I could have sworn I saw it move.

Chapter Three

A Strange Collection

I drove over to the house again straight after breakfast. There was a police car parked across the end of the street, blue and red lights splashing across the grey terraced houses. A skinny, bored looking copper stood there, resenting not being allowed to lean on the bonnet of his car. I pulled up and wound down my window.

"I'm sorry sir," he said, "the road's closed. There's been a fire in the night and the fire service are still making things safe."

"Was it number 19?" My stomach sank even before he answered.

"Might I ask why you would think that, sir? Were you here last night?"

"It's my grandfather's house. Well, it was. I suppose it's mine now." Not that I could prove it, if the deeds had been inside.

"I think you'd better talk to the sergeant, sir. You can park over there." He waved me to a small lay-by just past his car and spoke into his radio. I pulled in and walked back over to find a well-padded man in his mid-thirties had joined him.

"Good morning sir, can I ask why you were trying to reach this property?" he asked in the policeman's voice they use when talking professionally.

"It's my house. My grandfather died recently and left it to me, I was just going up to clear it out," I said, waving in that general direction. "Is there much damage?"

"I'm afraid so, sir. The neighbours' homes were very fortunate to escape with only minor damage, and by some miracle no-one was hurt. At what time did you leave the property last night, sir?"

"I'm not sure, about 5 o'clock? Why?"

"The first reports of fire came in at around midnight, so we will need to know where you were at that time."

"I'm staying in the Travelodge up the road," I waved in that direction. "I was there all night, I'm sure they'll tell you."

"We need to ask, sir," the sergeant said. "I'm sure you understand."

"We see all sorts in this job, sir," his junior added. The sergeant nodded.

"Look, can I go into the house? Is there anything left?" I asked.

"I'll escort you up there and take some details from you in case we need to speak to you again."

On the way, I kept craning my neck to catch a glimpse of the house, but the bends in the road and the trees on either side hid it from my view. The whole way the sergeant took notes and probed my story.

"Could it have been someone unhappy at being left out of the will, perhaps? If they couldn't have it, no-one could?" he asked.

"No, there was only me in his family. Well, apart from my father..." I hesitated.

"Your father, sir? Wouldn't he normally be in a direct line to inherit?"

"If anyone knew where he was, perhaps. He's hardly going to burn a house down to say hello after 30 years."

"I see." An estranged father, arson... He was salivating at the prospect of a major crime to investigate.

We rounded the corner, and I stumbled mid-step. It looked like someone had scooped the house out of the middle of the terrace. As the sergeant stated, the neighbouring houses were somehow undamaged. Someone had placed steel bars across the void where number 19 had stood, braced against the walls of the neighbours to prevent them falling into the gap. The fire fighters were rolling up their hoses. A few wisps of smoke curled from the rubble, but the fire was long since extinguished. The scent of wet ash filled the air.

Many people were gathered watching in dressing gowns and night-wear, glaring in my direction. I tried to ignore their angry muttering and introduced myself to one of the firemen.

"What happened?" I asked.

"We reckon it was deliberate," he said. "We're waiting on the in-vestigator to finish up, but if someone poured petrol through the letterbox and chucked in a firework, that'd do the trick."

"But how did it destroy everything?" I croaked. "Bricks don't burn, do they?"

"Fire's a strange beast. It must have been a scorcher to go up that fast but leave next door and the basement untouched. You know, I had a shout last week where a bloke had fallen asleep in his armchair smoking and the chair had gone up. Wasn't much left of him, but would you believe the carpet weren't even scorched?"

I nodded, and then my brain caught up with what he'd said. "The basement?"

"Yeah, the trapdoor's pretty warped, but a few whacks with a pry bar and we could check it looked OK down there. Small comfort, I guess."

How had I missed an entire basement the previous day? "What, er, did you find down there?" It came out sounding much more suspicious than I had intended. "I mean, it's my grandfather's place, I only just found out about it. I didn't get to go down there yet."

"There weren't much, and it might well be water-damaged now. From the hoses, you know? I'll see if he's done with his checks and whether he'll let you down."

The investigator pronounced himself satisfied, took a few last photographs of the damage, and then allowed us into the ruins of the house. The burnt and blackened root of the staircase smouldered in the centre of the plot and the firefighter pointed out the trapdoor which would have been in the cupboard under the stairs. He borrowed a torch from one of his colleagues and handed it to me. With his own, he led the way down the stone steps into the darkened basement.

The tight beams of our torches cast circles into the gloom, reflecting rough stone walls. A dirt floor glistened wet in the torch light, puddles grouping in the hollows. The smell of damp earth, smoke and musty neglect filled my nostrils as I stumbled down the last step. My torch light showed piles of cardboard boxes. Those sat on the bare floor looked soggy already, but the ones piled on top of them would stay dry long enough for me to salvage their contents.

The basement didn't go under the living room, though it extended back under the kitchen. The wall at the front was level with the stairs and contained a bookcase. As I looked through the boxes, a call came over the fireman's radio and he turned to me.

"You OK down here, mate?" the fireman said. "I shouldn't let you stay on your own really, but it's pretty solid down here, you're not in any danger."

"Hmm? Yeah, sure," I replied, fingering the documents in the first box I'd opened. It contained remnants of newspapers and magazines, the source of the cuttings I'd found upstairs. I crossed to the bookcase and shone my torch across the titles arrayed at eye-level. They were more occult books, except for an incongruous hardback edition of *Wisden's Cricketer's Almanac* from 1973. My grandfather had never been a cricket fan as far as I knew, and I pulled the book from the shelf. Or rather, I tried to. It didn't come free but tipped forward as if hinged, and a quiet click echoed around the damp basement. The entire bookcase sank slightly into the floor and moved away from me a fraction. A dim light shone out around the edge, suggesting space beyond.

I adjusted my glasses, stepped closer, and pushed. The shelves swung silently and revealed a room the same length as the living room above it, lit despite the lack of windows or working power. I looked around for a light source, but a set of shelves along the right-hand wall captured my attention instead. A jumble of jars ranging from an inch high to something that held a gallon or more filled the shelves. Each contained a cloudy liquid with shapes inside, indistinct in the low light. A slip of yellowed paper labelled each of them, further obscuring the contents. I picked up one the same size as a jam jar, the lid revealing it had once contained strawberry jam. As I moved it, the contents shifted and a cloud of particles rose inside like a snow globe, obscuring whatever might have been within. On the label I read:

{Pyxie vulgaris} Common Pixie
    Acq. J.W. c.1922 Avebury

Surely this was some kind of joke. I turned the jar around to examine its contents, but the snowstorm of debris hid it. I took another jar from the shelf, being careful not to joggle it. This one read:

{Fata sylva} Fairy (wood)
    Acq. H.W. 14th June 1967, Sand's End

With the gentlest of movements, the contents swam into view and I almost dropped the jar in surprise. It was a preserved specimen, such as you might see in a natural history museum under alcohol. But this was no snake or small rodent, this was a human form the size of a mouse, with a shock of bright red hair. That hair and the creature's tattered green clothes floated around in the fluid as the figure rotated. It had gossamer-thin wings flattened against its back, translucent and veined like dragonfly wings. There was no denying this looked exactly like a fairy.

Except for the sharp pointed teeth, exposed by a rictus grin. Those and the black beady eyes were more menacing than the story book creatures I had always imagined when someone mentioned the name 'fairy'. My heart thundered as I stared at the impossible sight.

"It's hard to comprehend, isn't it?" a voice behind me said.

Chapter Four

A Bizarre Society

I spun to face the speaker, a short, skinny, elderly man.

"But I assure you, Mr Williams, it's all real. I just wish you hadn't found it."

"Who the hell are you?" I shouted. "Get out of here!"

"You can call me Mr Green," he replied calmly. "And I have more right to be here than you do."

"Like hell you do, this was my grandfather's house, and he left it to me!"

He held up his palms in mock surrender, his rumpled suit hanging loose on his slight frame. "Ah, but you see this room was not his to give away. Our Society places some of its resources at the disposal of its members, but it never lets them pass out of our hands. They are rare, valuable, and until you blundered into the middle of this, very secret."

I couldn't manage anything more than incoherent stammering.

"It's a shame you have discovered this place, Mr Williams. It would have been much easier on you had you not." He ran a hand through his thinning red hair, flecked with grey.

I took a step towards him. "Is that a threat, Mr 'Green'?"

"Oh good heavens no," he said, "merely a regret. Neither I nor our Society bear you any ill will. Quite the opposite. But things will be much harder now."

"What on earth are you talking about? You're trying to tell me that this is real? You were playing a prank on an old man, taking advantage of him in his old age. Were you after money? He didn't have much, you know."

"Calm down, Mr Williams. Your grandfather recruited me into the Society, and I well remember how I once felt as you did. That I was being 'taken advantage of' as you suggest. We took nothing from him he didn't give freely, and that was never money."

"That's not what I meant, I don't care about that..." I stammered. "I just thought..."

"Perhaps we can discuss this somewhere more comfortable, Mr Williams? I'd be happy to explain if you were willing to listen calmly?" He managed not to make this sound patronising, but I had the distinct impression he was used to hiding his true opinion of someone behind a veneer of politeness.

"I'm not about to leave all this unattended, after what happened last night. Hold on, you didn't have something to do with that too, did you?"

"My, my. You are a suspicious one," he said. "No, Mr Williams, but we limited the destruction and protected the innocent from suffering because of our lapse."

"Lapse? What do you mean? And which innocent?"

"The neighbours are innocent in all of this, Mr Williams," he explained, cleaning his thick round glasses with an embroidered handkerchief. "And our lapse was in not collecting our property earlier, but we believed the protections were adequate. We know better now, but the important materials will now be safe. Come, I can explain better over coffee. The damp in here is not doing my lungs any good. Mr Blue?" He called this last over his shoulder towards the book-case-cum-hidden-door.

A man built like a brick wall, tall and wide, ducked under the lintel and grunted at me as he entered. He extended a spade of a hand for me to shake, which I did by force of habit as I cast my eyes over him. He wore grubby brown overalls and black steel-toed boots, as did the two smaller men who walked in after him. They carried bundles of corrugated cardboard which they unfolded into boxes, and tarpaulins which they spread on the floor. As they set up each box, Mr Blue (I didn't believe that was his name any more than I believed Green's was) carried jars from the shelves behind me and placed them inside. He set to work packing them reverentially with crunched up newspaper, which his colleagues brought from the boxes scattered around the rooms.

"Wait a minute, where are you taking all this?" I tried to protest.

"Somewhere where they can be better protected," Green explained. Blue grunted in agreement.

Over my continued questioning Green steered me to the door, up the stairs and blinking into the morning light. I wasn't sure why I'd followed him, but it felt the most natural thing to do. The neighbours had been allowed back into their homes, one of the fire engines had already left, and the other was pulling away. There was no sign of the police sergeant either. Doubtless he'd gone back to the station to start investigations into the absentee father with a grudge and a gallon of petrol.

Parked outside in the space vacated by the fire crews was a nondescript white van, with simple black lettering on the side: 'Green & Blue House Clearances'. Underneath in smaller letters it read: 'Fast, safe and discreet.' There was no phone number.

"We find it best to provide people with what they expect to see. You've had a fire, you need someone to clear the place, so we have a van outside to perform that precise duty. None of the neighbours will bat an eyelid, and nor would anyone else, should they be watching."

We walked back down the street to where I'd parked. The policeman at the end of the road was now leaning on the front of his car and didn't glance at us.

"Who would be watching?" I asked, as I unlocked my car and pulled open the door.

"Anyone," Green replied enigmatically, and he got into the passenger seat. The woodsy scent of his cologne was overpowering in the compact space.

Following his directions through a maze of residential roads, we ended up at a small parade of shops beside the river. Through the plate-glass windows of one, I could see a handful of people sipping from oversized china cups.

Once inside, Mr Green ordered a large cappuccino for himself and an Americano for me. "That is right, isn't it?" he checked, and I nodded. We took a seat in the window overlooking the Tyne Bridge and he sipped his coffee, sighing appreciation as he put the cup back in the saucer. There was a lengthy pause, broken only by the barista dropping a cup behind the counter. A sarcastic round of applause from a table in the corner greeted the shattering of china.

"Right, Mr Williams," Green said. "I think you've calmed down sufficiently for me to release you again." He then muttered something I didn't catch, and the serenity of disconnection, of being insulated by cotton wool from the worries I'd had before, vanished. Blood pounded in my ears, and I felt my muscles tighten as my anger and frustration returned. I shook my head to clear it.

"What the hell...?" I started, but a raised hand from the man across the table interrupted me.

"It was necessary to get you here and to allow us to continue our work. I hate to use magic on someone without permission, especially someone who is rightly angered, but desperate times... I plead for your forgiveness and understanding." His sincerity silenced me for a moment, no doubt as he intended. "Now I said I would explain and explain I shall. It's the least that I owe you. But where to start?"

"How about with what is going on?" My stunned silence was ended. "Who are you, who is this 'Society', what was my grandfather doing in that room?" I hesitated a moment. "And did you say 'magic' just now?"

Chapter Five

A Peculiar Secret

"I will answer your questions, but first you must understand something. What you are about to learn will not be easy to believe, but it will all be true — or at least as true as we know it to be." He locked eyes with me. "I will not lie to you today, I promise you that."

"OK…" I said.

"And I would urge you not to repeat anything you may learn today — or anything you saw in that house — to another living soul outside the Society. Anyone hearing what you had to say would question your sanity, and it's possible that the wrong 'people' might overhear something and bring you or your loved ones into danger."

Danger? Now that the fog in my head had lifted, I remembered I hadn't called Claire back last night. Was she at risk? Green anticipated my question.

"I'm sure your wife is fine, for now," he said none too reassuringly. "Or ex-wife, rather. But it would help me keep her that way if you tell her nothing."

"The divorce isn't final yet. Plus she knows I inherited the house and her lawyer will agitate for half of it!" I protested. "I can't keep this from her, you see that."

"I suppose she will need to know about the fire, but you can explain that everything was lost in it. You said you'd taken the book with you. Is it in your car at present?"

"No, I left it in the hotel this morning." Panic rose in my throat. "Is that safe? Should we...?" I leaped up, ready to fetch it.

He waved me back into my seat. "We have someone watching your room, it will be fine there for now. That book is the most valuable thing your grandfather worked on, more so than anything Mr Blue is transporting with his usual tender care."

I had a dozen more questions, but he asked me to wait. "Allow me to start at the beginning, Mr Williams. If I tell the story in the right order, it will be much simpler to comprehend, if not easier to believe." I nodded my assent and sipped my coffee. It was excellent, hot and strong without being bitter, and I took another sip as Green started his tale.

The Fae Defence Society (he explained) was set up in 1895, a time when science and technology had been unlocking the secrets of the world faster than ever. Leading physicists had even been quoted as saying that everything there was to be discovered had been. At the same time as science was rising to every challenge it was met with, religion was declining. People were embracing scientific progress, hearing news and opinions from around the world via telegraph and telegram, and many of them no longer saw the need for a reactionary institution to tell them what was right and wrong. This was the age of a new morality, one built on scientific ideals where the right action in any situation could be determined by logic alone.

Nevertheless, there were those who knew a larger truth. That outside science there were still things unexplored, mysteries unexplained. And while the eternal truth or otherwise of the existence of God was outside their abilities to explore, smaller mysteries were more easily probed. Since the dawning of mankind there had been myths and legends of innumerable creatures: dragons, chimeras, centaurs, fairies, goblins, genies. There were as many stories as there were storytellers. But some themes were constant, some ideas persisted across cultures: small, helpful (and hindering) sprites cropped up in the tales of every nation. Large mythical beasts, which needed the bravest and noblest knight or warrior to slay, appeared across the globe. Every village around the world had at least one place reputed to be haunted. And if there was a child anywhere who wasn't warned against going into the woods alone at night for fear of the vicious 'boogeyman', then they were rare indeed.

A group of men and women gathered with the goal of studying these myths and stories, teasing out the common factors and determining the truth that they contained. Thus began the 'Fae Defence Society.'

At this point I interrupted to ask whether it was wise to talk about it here in public. Green nodded, and I realised that the background noise of the coffee shop had dropped away. No longer could I hear the hum of conversation at nearby tables, and when someone stirred their drink, I didn't hear the tinkle of the spoon in the cup.

"How did you...?" I stammered.

"A simple spell," he said matter-of-factly, and continued his story.

These first few men and women had determined that not only were there common parts of these stories which repeated, but that a good many of the stories had a basis in truth. The tricky part was trying to tease apart the layers of myth to reveal the nugget of truth at the centre.

"One example," he said. "Are you familiar with the story of the cobbler and the elves?"

"The one where the elves come out at night to make shoes to save his family? Are you saying it's true?"

"More or less. We've learned a few things about elves over the years and they wouldn't do anything from the kindness of their hearts, or what passes for hearts. We suspect that any shoes they made would have been enchanted to serve their own purposes."

"I'm sorry," I laughed. "Magic boots?"

Green wasn't laughing. "You really must put aside your memories of childish fairy tales, Mr Williams. Magic always has a price, and it's rarely one you want to pay."

"But you're doing it right now!" I said.

"A trifling spell," he said. "But in the case of the elves, they would have relished the opportunity to put enchantments onto shoes or boots that would be sold far and wide. When you were out working in the fields or walking through the forest, they could lead your steps astray very easily. A lost child in the woods, I needn't explain how vulnerable they would be to an attack..."

I swallowed hard. Suddenly there wasn't anything amusing about magical footwear.

"And even an adult, if you can lure them into the right place, could be easy prey. Believe me, you do not want to find yourself among standing stones on the wrong day of the year!"

"And all this got turned into a happy tale of a down-at-heel shoemaker, leaving out saucers of milk?" I asked.

"Did you ever read the original fairy stories collected by the brothers Grimm?"

"I think I saw that book once, when I was a kid," I replied. "My Grandad had a copy."

"By the time they became popular, they were safe for children to read. Successive retellings made them kinder and gentler. But the earlier editions, the first in particular, were much more accurate records of the folk tales passed from generation to generation. Much gorier, much nastier, much scarier and much closer to the truth. Even then, they only scratched the surface of how evil that world can be. Hence the need for an organised defence."

"Fairy tales are true?" I asked.

"No, not for the most part. Cinderella for example is an utter fiction. A girl oppressed like that would naturally dream of a fairy godmother, a magic carriage and fine clothes, not to mention a prince who'd take her away from her poor life. But things like that don't happen to people in reality."

"Neither do elves making shoes, or picking off kids in the woods..." I countered.

"I think you'll find, Mr Williams, that wonderful things don't happen as often as we want, but terrible things are a lot more common than we like."

"A bit pessimistic. I think you'll find I've had a good life, thank you. My glass is half full."

He smiled. "A pessimist is just a realist with life experience. As you spend more time within the Society, I assure you you'll gain that experience rather quickly."

"I'm not planning to spend any time in your 'Society'," I countered. "I have no interest in joining some fairy spotters club."

"You don't understand," he replied. "Call it a legacy, but you're destined to. It's a shame your grandfather wasn't able to introduce you, but I must do it and quickly I'm afraid. You must come with me now, Richard Williams."

CHAPTER SIX

A REMARKABLE OFFICE

As Mr Green spoke, he rose from his seat and beckoned me to follow. Despite my earlier protestations, I felt compelled to obey him again. As he walked he appeared tired, and somehow shorter. I turned to follow him past the barista loading cups into the dishwasher and towards a door marked 'Employees Only'. Green twisted the doorknob, pushed the door open and stepped through into what should have been a compact storage room. Instead, a long dark corridor stretched ahead of us into the distance, descending as it went.

My surprise must have been clear on my face as Green chuckled. "We have a few entrances scattered around, but it never hurts to open a fresh one no-one else knows about from time to time."

"Entrances to what?" I asked.

"You'll see soon enough," he replied, and set off along the corridor. A slight blue glow preceded us along the darkened path, illuminating a stone floor beneath our feet. The glow didn't extend more than a few feet in the direction we were heading, nor far enough to make out the walls. I stretched a hand out and touched smooth stone, cold and sightly greasy under my fingers.

"You must learn not to touch," Green rebuked me. "Some things you will encounter don't take kindly to probing fingers." I snatched my hand back and wiped it on my jeans, as if contaminated. "You're all right in here, but you might find the walls... disconcerting as we pass through the Divide."

His silhouette shimmered as if I were viewing him through water before settling back to normal.

"Mind your step," he warned me. "It can feel a little peculiar."

I walked forward.

You know that feeling when you stand up too fast, and the blood rushes away from your head? You're dizzy, your heart lurches to pump blood back up, your ears ring, and you reach out to grab something for support. That's what happened as I took that step. The dim light swam before my eyes, then brightened painfully. My inner ears and stomach told me I was falling, and I reached out an arm to steady myself. I clutched Mr Green's arm through the sleeve of his jacket. His arm was like twigs, gnarled and fragile in my grasp. The dizziness passed, I released my grip and squinted into the light.

We were in a room four metres on each side, with a solid white marble floor and tiled floor-to-ceiling with large white marble slabs. The ceiling itself was far above, its exact distance hard to judge as it formed the only source of light, diffuse yet bright and casting no shadows. I turned around. The heavy metal door behind us reminded me of one you might see on a boat, made of riveted thick steel with a wheel in the centre which turned as I watched. The door clanged shut, and the wheel stopped turning.

"All good?" Mr Green said. "You'll get used to it, in time."

"Where *are* we?" I asked, my reluctance to ask stupid questions forgotten.

"The offices of the Society. We have many entrances, but they all lead here. I'm sure you can't imagine the trouble we'd have if we needed a secure reception room for each doorway, so we combine them all here."

"But why does it look like a... Turkish bath?" I said.

"Ah, well, it cleans easily you see. Some of our... guests aren't as welcome as you are, so we have to take measures."

"You mean, you kill people in here?" I gasped.

"Oh no, if they can get in here uninvited, then they're almost never people," he replied in a matter-of-fact tone. "And we can check." He waved a hand to the ceiling, which turned a deep red and displayed a circular pattern of strange symbols. "If you were one of our more unwelcome visitors, you'd be in considerable pain now." He smiled. I found it hard to return the grin. With only red light suffusing the room, he looked menacing. The light on the walls rippled, giving the impression of flowing blood. With another wave, Green returned the ceiling to its white hue. "Shall we go on?" he asked.

I couldn't see where we'd go. There was only one door, and we'd just come through it. Turning his hand in mid-air as if operating a doorknob, Green smiled as the central wheel spun and the door swung towards us. There was no stone-clad corridor on the other side, no sign of the long dark hallway we'd just traversed, but an office reception desk, large and ancient, remarkable only in its ordinariness. An old woman sat behind it, busy with file folders and a mountain of paper. The room was otherwise unfurnished, save for a few oil painted portraits that were probably a hundred years old. I'd no idea what I'd been expecting, but a room full of guttering candles, pentagrams and hooded figures chanting would have been less surprising than this.

"Good morning Janice," Green said to the woman behind the desk.

"Welcome back, Mr Green, and hello Mr Williams, nice to have you with us," Janice replied. A soft chime sounded, and she asked to be excused. She pulled a round, flat brass dish towards her with both hands and peered into it. Her lips moved silently for a few moments before she pushed the dish away again and spoke out loud. "Mr Green, Mr Blue said that everything has been secured, and he's taking it to Liverpool." I realised that her desk had no telephone, and that whatever she'd just done, that dish must have taken the place of one.

"Thank you, Janice," Mr Green said. He placed one hand on my back and, with his other hand outstretched, guided me towards a more traditional office door beyond the reception desk. I let him propel me along another corridor, this one panelled in black oak with worn green carpet underfoot. Small ornate lamps hung on either side every few feet, between half-panelled doors with frosted glass. Names were imprinted on the glass of each one in gold lettering. For all I could tell, I was in a perfectly ordinary office building such as any old company might own in a major city. A thought occurred to me.

"Where are we, now? We didn't walk far down that corridor, but I guess we're not under that coffee shop or its neighbours..."

"We're in London, Mr Williams, in as far as we are anywhere. This is the 13th floor of a rather ugly old building on the banks of the Thames, in fact."

"Newcastle, you mean. The Tyne."

He shook his head.

"And don't most buildings skip the 13th floor?" I asked. Whenever I'd visited an office tower or large hotel, the lift buttons had gone from 12 straight to 14.

"Indeed, so no-one will miss this one!" he replied.

"But we can't be 13 floors up, we travelled downhill from ground level..." If we had travelled from Newcastle to London in the blink of an eye, we could certainly rise a few hundred feet without difficulty. No wonder I'd felt dizzy. "Oh, right," I finished.

"And besides, the building no longer exists anyway," Green continued, ignoring my moment of stupidity.

"What?"

"We preserved this floor of the building when it came time to demolish it. We had spent a while customising it to our needs, and you know what a hassle it is to move."

"But that's impossible," I protested. Green sighed.

"I thought we would be past that by now. Many things thought impossible have long been commonplace. The ability to see things occurring at a great distance away, talk to loved ones in another country, fly like the birds, these were all thought impossible until someone came up with the television, telephone or aeroplanes."

"But those are scientific, I mean we can explain and understand them, reproduce them. They make sense!" I argued.

"Can you build an aeroplane, Mr Williams? Or explain how a television works? I doubt it, not in detail at any rate. They work as if by magic, and they would be described as such by our ancestors. Would you be happier if I said that the office you see only exists because we preserved it in a space-time bubble maintained in isolation from the ongoing entropy of the universe? Or would that be just as 'impossible' to you?"

"But we don't know how to do that, it *is* impossible!"

Mr Green muttered that he would show me proof of his claims and opened one of the office doors. Inside was a time capsule from the 1950s. A typewriter stood on the heavy wooden desk, denting the green leather inlay. Behind the desk stood a matching chair, and a filing cabinet in one corner had a terracotta plant pot on top of it, empty apart from a few grey and brittle leaves hanging over the sides. A coat rack, an umbrella stand and a wastepaper basket completed the museum exhibit. I barely took it in, however, as the vast picture window on the wall opposite the door drew my attention.

I looked out over London. There could be no doubt that we were there, and several floors above ground level. The river snaked across the centre of the vista, glistening silver in the early evening sun. I checked my watch to confirm it was still morning and then looked back into the orange glow of an imminent sunset. We were on the North bank of the Thames, somewhere between the Embankment and St. Paul's Cathedral, but I couldn't see the skyline I expected. There was no Shard, in fact several tower blocks and skyscrapers were notably absent. I craned my neck to look towards Parliament — at least that was there — but the London Eye was missing! I swung my eyes along the river, pressing my face to the glass. Barges with large grey sails were tacking up and down the river's course, rather than the usual tourist boats or ferries. The longer I looked, the more oddities I noticed. The roads on this side of the river teemed with horses pulling carts and carriages I was sure belonged in Victorian times. On the other were a handful of cars from the 1940s. A quiet voice spoke behind me.

"I mentioned we had retained this floor when the building that housed it was demolished. As you can imagine, without that anchor it is rather tricky to keep us in a particular time period. But we should get going. I need to get you prepared."

CHAPTER SEVEN

A TERRIFYING DEMONSTRATION

"Prepared for what?" I dragged myself away from the patchwork image of London through the ages and followed Green along the corridor. We arrived in front of a much heavier oak door that lacked the pane of glass this time. An engraved brass plaque took the place of the gold letters:

Laboratory No. 3
Unauthorised Access Prohibited
Magical Threat Level 4 and higher

Mr Green didn't even glance at this warning, but opened the door and stepped through. I followed him into a windowless room like the entrance room we'd arrived in earlier. The same diffuse light emanated from the ceiling, but the walls and floor were simple white porcelain instead of marble. Where the entryway had put me in mind of a swimming pool or shower room, this one reminded me of a station toilet right down to the same smell of antiseptic. Two elderly men in white lab coats pushed a large square shape under a blanket into the room, from which emanated the noise of heavy breathing. From an anteroom in one corner, an attractive younger woman with dark skin, curly black hair and a crisp white lab coat over bright red trousers walked into the centre of the room. She nodded a greeting to Green and peered at me for a moment, before she gestured to someone behind me.

From a chair in the room's corner, a tiny shrivelled figure crawled towards the door. They were only five feet tall, but their pronounced stoop made them appear much shorter. Rake-thin and with papery skin wrinkled and sallow, they looked terminally ill. It surprised me to see them outside a hospital bed, let alone dragging their feet around this tiled room. I looked over at Mr Green, but he shook his head to discourage my questions. The figure placed both hands on the door as high as he (no, now I was sure it was she) could reach, and took a deep, rasping breath. A deep green glow started between her hands, brightening and getting lighter in hue as it spread across the entire door. Just as it became too bright to look at, it reached the door frame and flowed into the cracks between the frame and the door, filling the gap. The figure slumped, and for an instant I thought she had died. But she drew a few shallow gasps of breath which caused her to cough wetly, and she shuffled back towards her straight-backed chair, leaning on the wall for support. I stepped towards her to help, but Mr Green grabbed my arm and stopped me before turning his attention to the two white coated men.

"I believe we are ready, gentlemen?" he said. The men I presumed were scientists, or this place's equivalent looked at each other, and then at the woman between them. She was looking straight at Mr Green and annoyance flashed across her face for an instant before she nodded to them to continue. With that, one of them reached over and pulled back the blanket.

I screamed.

A huge cage sat on castors, the bars arcing with greasy lightning. Inside was a hairless creature the size of a dog. Its skin was a vile colour somewhere between green and black, suggesting putrefaction. In texture, it resembled flaking paint with lighter coloured flesh beneath, and there were flecks of shed skin around it on the floor. Its legs were thick and powerful, muscles rippling beneath that cracked skin. Instead of paws it had long toes, tipped with wet-looking black claws that scraped across the wooden base of the cage. There were deep gouges where it had tried to claw its way out. It had holes in the sides of its head where its ears should be. And its eyes — I stepped back in horror at the sight — they were full of malevolence, all of it directed straight at me. I took in the sight of those jet black irises that blended into the pupils. It looked deep inside me, reading my fears and stoking my terror. My heart pounded in my chest and I wanted to flee, but I was certain that if it wanted to pursue me, it would. I wasn't confident that the cage could contain it.

With difficulty, I broke eye contact and found my eyes drawn to its mouth, a long wide slit slashed deep along the head. The mouth fell open revealing black gums studded with triangular shark-like teeth, each one long enough to pierce my flesh. Thick green drool dripped from its gaping maw as it breathed loudly in the quiet room, the mouth opening wider and wider until its head was sure to split open. My eyes were drawn back to the intelligent hatred in its eyes. This couldn't be a mere animal. It was too aware, too deliberately cunning to be mistaken for a dumb creature of instinct.

"We captured this a few hours ago. It was sniffing around your hotel."

Mr Green's words shook me from my panic for a moment until I realised what he was implying. "Th-that... thing was after m-me?" I stammered, dry-mouthed.

"Yes," Green replied. "That is why I came to meet you at the house, Mr Williams. It was necessary to protect you as much as our property. Once you started to investigate, to find and handle the items you did, you broke the masking charms and revealed yourself to them. They marked you." I heard the capital letters. "From that moment, you were in danger."

I stood there trembling, unable to tear my eyes from the horrifying creature, now pacing from side to side in the confines of its cage. At one point it grazed the bars and a bolt of oily-blue electricity arced into its side with a deafening crack. It let loose a howling scream that chilled my blood and sent icy shivers down my spine. Even Mr Green twitched, although he covered it up with dignity. It was the sound of a nightmare, a primal cry of anguish and pain, and the echo from the smooth walls amplified the terrifying effect. I felt no sympathy for this thing in the cage, but the noise it made touched the deep primitive part of me that said 'be afraid', and I was powerless to resist.

As the echoes died away, I reassured Mr Green that he had nothing to fear from me revealing his secrets. I could not stop shaking, cold sweat pooled in the small of my back and my stomach churned. Mr

Green laid a sympathetic hand on my shoulder and tried to calm me.

"We can protect you, but the more time you spend in our world, the more dangerous it will become."

"Right, so let me go, you'll never see me again!" I almost begged.

"I wish I could. This is your legacy, you were always destined to join this fight. If I could free you from that burden then I would, but it's impossible."

"Like hell it is, let me out of here. I'll keep your secrets, but I will not put myself into danger for you or anyone else! You will not keep me here against my will, and I will not help you. You'll have to find someone else to fight these... abominations," I finished, gesturing at the creature. It looked up at me and growled, a sound that caused every hair on my head to stand upright. I fought the crazy urge to apologise to it.

"I'm sorry to hear that, Mr Williams. But you see we have only very limited resources these days, and can only extend our protection to, shall we say, high value individuals? If you won't help us, then I'm afraid we can't help you either. No matter what might... come up." He glanced at the cage as he said that, and I caught his meaning.

"Either I help you, or you hang me out to dry?" I spat. "Where do you get off threatening me like that?" The creature grew more agitated as I did, and threw itself against the bars, triggering another electrical blast and another howl which caused me to jump. "You only protect me if I expose myself to a greater danger? Some deal that is!"

Mr Green had doubtless assumed I'd be clamouring to be part of their club. The two older men were trying not to meet either his or my eyes as they covered up the cage again and wheeled it away. The woman bit her lip to hide a smirk.

"But, your destiny…" Green began, before he saw my look. "Very well, we'll take care of that one, and it's possible you won't be followed any further. We can make sure you leave Newcastle in safety." An idea occurred to him. "But let me show you a means to protect yourself, at least. Then you can go home and make your decision in your own time. Perhaps you'll feel different after you've seen what we can offer."

Chapter Eight

A Powerful Lesson

"I won't change my mind, I promise you that now," I said.

Green didn't reply, but nodded to the youthful woman who had now lost the battle to hide her smile. "I'm Tina. Tina Black," she introduced herself. She retrieved a few items from a table against the far wall and handed them to me. First, there was a small Art Deco styled perfume atomiser with a rubber bulb and a nozzle on the top. Squeezing the bulb generated a fine mist of liquid and the odour of cinnamon. Mr Green tutted, and I remembered his advice not to touch things. Second, I picked up a long silver hatpin with a purple glass bead at the end. The interior of the bead swirled and writhed when viewed out of the corner of my eye, but on looking at it directly it resembled the cheap costume jewellery it no doubt was. Last, a small powder-compact decorated with an Art Deco pattern to match the atomiser.

"What's with the old lady stuff?" I asked.

"The spray reveals the presence of the Fae," the woman stated. "If you think something's there, spray that into the general area, and it'll show up for a few moments, giving you time to strike. Or run," she added, off Green's glare.

"Wait, so these things are invisible?" I asked.

"You don't think something like that would still be a secret if anyone could see it, do you?" She laughed. "Of course they're invisible to most people. Except under exceptional circumstances."

"Cats can sense them," Green said, "that's why they suddenly take off from a room for no reason."

"But I could see that one," I said.

"There are ways to make them visible permanently," she replied, "for research or preservation purposes. But that's a little advanced, so we'll stick with the spray for now. Let's give it a test run." She took an empty cage from the table and held it in front of her at arm's length. "Go on," she urged me. Certain I was the target of a practical joke, I raised the atomiser to the level of the cage, and pressed the bulb.

The fine mist spread out from the nozzle and hung in the air for a moment. Then, as if caught in a draught, it darted to the back left corner of its cage and coalesced into the outline of a tiny figure crouched in the corner. As the liquid faded from sight, it left an after image of a fairy identical to the one I'd seen in that jar in the basement, only this one was alive. When it realised I could see it, it turned to look at me, and made a high-pitched, plaintive sound. I was sure that it was speaking intelligent words, but any meaning was indistinguishable, like a conversation in a noisy room. After about twenty seconds it faded from view again, and so did the sound of its chattering. The sense of words just missed, lingered.

"Excellent," the woman said. "You need not be precise with the aim, anything within a few feet should be good enough. Once you can observe your adversary, what do you do about it? That's where the powder comes in."

I opened the powder-compact to find a red-green dust which shimmered in the light. "Do I blow this in its face too?" I asked.

"No, you eat it," she replied. "That'll unlock your magical abilities, but it needs activating first. Take the needle and prick your finger. I'd advise the little finger. You might find that easier to deal with. Are you right-handed?" I nodded. "Then the left hand would be best, just a few drops will do." I held the powder-compact in my left hand and aimed the hatpin at my finger. Was I really going to do this, based on the urging of someone I had just met? It took a while to get up the nerve to stab myself deliberately, but when I did I saw a flash from the glass bead at the pin's head. A drop of bright red blood formed on my fingertip.

"Very good, now drip it onto the powder in the compact." I held my little finger over the powder and waited for a few drops of my blood to land on it. As each one did, it sizzled as if hitting a hot surface, and solidified into a jet black blob. After three drops she told me to stop. "Now, swallow those pills you've created, and hang on to your hat!" she said.

As I dry-swallowed the first pellet, I sensed a gentle wave of energy pass into my core like drinking iced water and feeling it all the way down. The second pill had a greater effect, and the third left me full of bottled lightning, ready to break out of me at any moment. I wasn't sure whether I was containing the power, or it was choosing to remain inside me for the time being. The energy pulsed inside me like waves on a beach.

"Now, you need to control it, ride the surges as they come and go," my teacher said. "As each one rises, pull up, and as it recedes, push away until you get it to a point you sense you cannot control it, then aim at the cage. It might help to point your hands at it." I did as she said, a sense of euphoria growing as I controlled the waves of power. This reminded me of pushing faster on a swing by pumping my legs. If I timed it right, I could build the waves higher and higher until they threatened to break over me. I looked at her in amazement. She smiled at me, and waving her hands over the cage, muttered something under her breath. The tiny creature I'd glimpsed earlier reappeared, and I almost lost control of the energy inside me at the sight.

It sensed the power and retreated to the far side of the cage.

"Imagine a thin silver layer around your body, like a wetsuit or a suit of armour," Tina said. "And recite the following words." She spoke a curious string of sounds which sounded strangely familiar, as if I'd once understood what they meant but had forgotten.

I closed my eyes and breathed deeply, visualising a shimmering protective skin around myself. I repeated the sounds Tina had made as best I could recall them, as they threatened to slip from my mind if I lost concentration. A greasy electricity slithered over my skin and I suppressed a shudder, before imagining the bubble expanding so as not to touch my skin.

"That's good!" she said. "You're already getting the idea. Now expand it into a sphere around yourself and see if you can sustain it while you open your eyes. You're not much use if you're blinded whenever you do something." I pictured a sphere of glowing light around me, and with a final deep breath I slowly opened my eyes.

To my surprise, I saw a tenuous bubble around my body, exactly where I'd pictured. It resembled a soap bubble with dancing rainbow patterns slipping over the surface, and as I lost my concentration, it burst like one.

"Oh!" I gasped, as the energy that had coursed through me vanished.

"You almost had it there. Have another try, but without closing your eyes."

"Will it hurt the creature?" I asked. I didn't believe something that small was dangerous, and I was reluctant to injure something defenceless.

"No, this is just a repelling spell. Now focus," Tina said.

This time I kept my emotions under control, and brought the shield in close behind me to extend the front out away from me, so it resembled a rugby ball. As it neared the cage, the creature drew back, squeaking and tumbling in its eagerness to get away. The front of the bubble passed through the bars, and the animal inside tried to climb to the top of the cage to escape. Just before it touched, Tina stopped me. I released my grip on the bubble around me and sensed it pop, leaving the hair on my head tingling.

"I did it! That was actual magic?" I said and then overwhelmed by dizziness and fatigue, I slumped to the floor. "Oh, wow, that was... Wow," I muttered. "That was something else," I finished.

"That was good, Mr Williams," Mr Green said.

Tina was more effusive. "That was bloody brilliant!" she cried. I looked up with a smile, taking all my energy to do so. "For a first time, anyway," she continued, subdued by a glare from Mr Green.

The dizziness was fading, but the fingers on my left hand were throbbing. I flexed them and they were stiff, as if I'd fallen asleep on them. My tutor noticed my gaze and explained. "That's magic, for you. It takes a toll at the best of times. You'll get the feeling back in a few minutes this time, but it'll get harder and take longer the more you do. There's always a cost." Now I knew why Mr Green had looked tired when we had left the coffee shop after his 'trifling spell'. I looked around at the woman who'd sealed the door. She was bent in her chair, smiling sympathetically, if weakly, at me. As I struggled to my feet, she did likewise, before being interrupted by a fit of coughing that racked her frail body. I lacked the strength to go over to help her and noticed that no-one else moved either.

My mind was reeling from what I'd experienced. Those strange creatures were real, as was magic. The strange rush of energy flowing through me had been euphoric, and now that it had subsided I wanted more.

Chapter Nine

A Welcome Return

As I shook Ms Black's hand and thanked her, the tired old woman shuffled back to the door and released the protective charm she'd applied to it. Mr Green guided me along the corridor to a small seating area where someone had produced a pot of tea, two delicate china cups on saucers, and a small jug of hot milk. There was also a plate of biscuits.

After a few minutes of silence, Green broached the subject again. "Frankly, Mr Williams, we need you. Losing your grandfather hurt us, and you will be more than capable of continuing his work. These abilities run in families. Magic is literally 'in the blood', and that makes you valuable." I glanced at my aching hand and tried to imagine what I could do for these people.

"I told you, I want nothing to do with all this," I replied. That taste of power had been tantalising, and I wished to learn more about this unseen world around us, but... "I have a job, a life, I don't want this. You can have the book back," I conceded, "and anything else I might have that is useful. But then I leave and go back to my old life."

"Is there nothing I can say that would convince you? I hoped an appeal to your curiosity might have swayed you, if self-preservation was not sufficient."

"No, I've seen more than enough of this world," I said. In truth I was still tempted, but the terror at the sight of that caged creature had more than outweighed my curiosity.

He sighed. "Very well, I shall take you back to the hotel to gather your things, and you can go home."

We walked in silence along the corridor and I took a last look at the view as we passed an open office. Night had fallen on one side of the river now, but the other lay in full sun. The flickering of the streetlights on the dark side suggested it was a not a recent view. When we reached the front desk, Mr Green opened the door into the marble-tiled arrival room.

"If I might get your hotel key card?" he asked me. "We need something tied to the location we wish to visit, to prime the Divide." I handed it over, interested to see more magic in action. Green pulled a small ornate silver folding knife from his jacket pocket and shaved a sliver of plastic from the card before handing it back. This he placed in a small niche to the side of the door, before adding a few pinches of a grey-blue powder from a crystal-cut jar. He pulled a cheap plastic lighter from his pocket, clicked it and touched the flame to the powder, which vanished in a dazzling flash. A cloud of sickly smoke rose to the ceiling, leaving a thin ash residue in the tray. He opened the door with a gesture and beckoned me forward.

Again, I felt that moment of disorientation, of dizziness, but this time I didn't stumble. The black corridor was shorter this time, we reached a plain wooden door within a few moments and Mr Green motioned for me to open it. I stepped through and found myself behind the hotel bar. On the door behind me was a sign reading 'Employees only'. Once we were both through, I closed the door and opened it again to reveal a storage room jammed with boxes of crisp packets. I marvelled for a moment, before someone called "Excuse me, that's private!" Muttering our apologies, we headed for my room.

Once there, I handed Green my grandfather's book, and he flicked through it. "I hope it helps you," I said, to break the awkward silence that had followed us since we left the offices. "Good luck, I guess."

"Thank you. Are you sure you won't reconsider?"

"Absolutely." I wouldn't betray any sense of regret at passing up the knowledge and secrets I'd seen a glimpse of that day.

"Then I shall wish you well, and a long and happy life, Mr Williams," he said, offering his hand to shake.

"Say, could you give me a lift back home? The train's not the most convenient way..." I asked. "Hang on, my car's still at that coffee shop!"

"You'll find it in the car park outside the hotel. And no, I don't think we should convey you to your home. Each use of magic attracts attention, and the closer to your home the greater the risk."

"Right, yes," I agreed.

"Oh, and don't worry about the house and the fire, I think you'll find the authorities are quite satisfied with the results of their enquiries," he added with a twinkle in his eye.

While I checked out of the hotel, my phone beeped, informing me I'd missed several calls and messages while I had been in the offices. Evidently getting phone service in an office trapped in a bubble hovering over a bygone London did not feature among their magical abilities.

All the messages had come from my office. They'd granted me a few days off on compassionate grounds, on the understanding I'd be available by phone in case of emergencies. I knew my colleagues wouldn't bother me unless they were stuck, but my boss was such a micro-manager that I could expect a few calls a day from him 'just to check a few details'. I gritted my teeth and checked the messages. Sure enough, he wanted to check whether I'd taken care of a particular issue before I left. I dashed out a text assuring him that not only had I finished the paperwork in question but had handed it to him in person. No doubt he'd just been unable to find it among the chaos on his desk.

I next called Claire and immediately regretted it.

"Where have you been? I've been trying to reach you all day." she said.

"Sorry, it's been a bit of a nightmare actually," I began.

"I was hoping you'd be able to pick me up from the hospital."

Memories of our last trip to the hospital rose unbidden. The scent of antiseptic and blood. "What's happened? Are you OK?"

"Of course I am. It was those routine tests I told you about. So you're not nearby?"

"I'm still in Newcastle, remember? Grandad's house?" I released the breath I hadn't realised I was holding.

"I've had a lot on my mind, you know. How is it?"

"Burned down," I replied. "The police think it was arson."

"Oh my God, are you OK?"

"It happened overnight, I wasn't there. And no-one got hurt, luckily. Although the neighbours had to be evacuated and hate me now."

"That was your inheritance. Will the insurance still pay out?" she asked.

I thought quickly. "The solicitors said he hadn't insured it, so it's likely we'll get nothing." Hoping that was the last lie I'd have to tell her, I assured her I'd call her again soon and hung up. At least she had been too distracted to ask about the divorce papers.

Messrs Green and Blue had left me my grandfather's hand-bound books I'd collected that first day. They looked very smart on the bookcase at home and I planned to read my way through them in the evenings, glad of the connection to him.

I'd found the powder-compact, atomiser and hat pin still in my jacket pocket after I got back, and another pocket yielded up the dictaphone and its tiny cassette. I put the former in a drawer in the kitchen, placed fresh batteries into the tape recorder and pressed play.

The recording started with a clattering sound as someone put the recorder on a table, and then a murmur of speech, too quiet to understand. I turned up the volume only to hear my grandfather's voice booming out of the speaker.

"Ask him to describe what happened," he said. I fumbled the volume back down again and another voice spoke in what I took to be Arabic. In the pause that followed came the indistinct voices again, and a flapping sound which triggered memories of camping holidays and the tent flap slapping in the wind. A third hesitant voice cut in, uncertain about what he was saying, or if he should speak at all. Then the second voice was back, translating what he had said.

"He says he was setting up his camp for the night, a few months ago. He was putting up the tents, and his wife was cooking at the fire. His son was tying up the goats while his daughter was playing a game in the sand."

"Was it dark? Did he see anyone else around?" my grandfather urged. Another exchange in Arabic and then the reply in English.

"No, the moon was full. He could see for miles in any direction and no-one was there. He says this is normal, they are often alone when they camp."

"I see. Please go on." He spoke these last words louder and slower, I smiled at the Englishman abroad always assuming the locals will understand him if he does that. Then I remembered that this was my grandfather, out in the deserts of who-knew-where, interviewing a Bedouin traveller. I looked at the cassette through the plastic window on the player. It bore the date 17th October 1976. That long ago, and he'd never mentioned travelling after his time in the army during the war.

"He says he heard a song from the sand. An old song, one his grandmother used to sing. He said it was..." Another back-and-forth in Arabic. "Yes, he says it was her singing. Even though she was gone for years, it was still her." The third voice broke in at this point.

"She call me," he said in English, his accent thick but the words clear.

"He says she sang to him, and called to him, but he did not go to her. He knew it was a spirit, a *dzokhim*. When he called his family to him, to get into the tent, his daughter did not come." I suspected what was coming next, but I couldn't turn off the recorder. "When he took a branch from the fire and went to where she had been tending the goats, he saw her shoes in the middle of a circle drawn in the sand. He knew then the *dzokhim* had taken her."

"He didn't go looking for her? She might have just wandered off!"

"Yes, he looked, but there were no footprints. Just hers leading from the camp to her shoes, and then nothing. She was taken, sir, you can be sure of that."

There was a lengthy silence, only broken by muffled sobs, the Bedouin unable to stifle his tears.

"*Shukran. Ana a'sef.*" My grandfather's voice again, low and sympathetic. "Has he told this story to the authorities? If they understood, they wouldn't be blaming him for..."

"No, he does not dare to speak to them of this, the old stories are not believed by... good-minded people."

"But would he not be better off if they thought he were mad, rather than a murderer?"

"As a madman he would still be a murderer, sir. And his family would be shunned. This way, maybe they can still be forgiven."

"But I could speak to them on his behalf, explain the truth..."

"No!" Both men shouted at once. "Please sir, no," the interpreter continued. "You would make it more difficult for him, your people are not trusted here. He only agreed to speak to you because he remembers his father told him stories about your father."

The tape ran out. My great grandfather had been part of this too? Was it truly a family legacy, as Mr Green had implied? If it was, my no-good father had already broken the chain. I sat there musing for a while, before I decided to distract myself and took a book from the bookcase next to me to read for a while. A small slip of yellowed paper fell out of the back. In small, neat handwriting that wasn't my grandfather's it read:

If ever you change your mind and wish to contact us, burn this paper. Green.

He must have slipped it in there when they returned the car and forgotten to mention it to me. I repurposed the slip of paper as a bookmark and resolved to think no more about it. Something I was to find harder to do than I imagined.

Chapter Ten

A Fateful Decision

My first day back at work was not pleasant. Strange dreams had tormented my sleep, and even a half-dozen coffees weren't enough to keep me alert. By the afternoon I was ready to go back home, and the caffeine had made me irritable. My boss still micro-managed me at every opportunity, and in my sleep-deprived state it was only a matter of time before I made a stupid mistake. It wasn't a major slip up, and I would have solved it before it caused any actual problems, but naturally he spotted it first.

The subsequent 'I'm just disappointed' speech came in an even more patronising tone than usual. A combination of broken sleep, dreams about monsters both real and imagined, and a surfeit of foul tasting vending machine coffee boiled over inside me. I snapped at him, he sniped back, and before I knew what was happening, we were in a full-blown shouting match in the middle of the office. At the end of it, he told me to go home and calm down. I resisted the temptation to resign there and then, and stomped out. After another night's fitful sleep I called in sick the next morning. I think my boss was as relieved as I was, and when I returned the following day I mumbled an apology and said something about not being myself. He agreed my behaviour must have been because of whatever 'bug' I was coming down with, and he made a show of playing the bigger man and accepting my apology in front of everyone. I swallowed my pride, sat at my desk and fumed.

I found it impossible to concentrate. My mind constantly wandered back to the remarkable things I'd seen: the 'Divide' that let you go anywhere you wished, the view over London from a building long since demolished that revealed ever-changing times and seasons as you watched. Even the creatures were less terrifying with the benefit of hindsight.

Then there was that rush of power when I'd used magic myself for the first time. It had burned like fire through every inch of my body. I'd loved the sensation I was able to do anything, if I just knew how to focus it. I resisted the truth for a while, but had to admit I missed that experience. I wanted to experience that energy, that potential, again. It didn't help that my boss was dogging my every footstep even closer than before. I think my outburst and later apology had given him hope I'd screw up again, and he could assert his dominance over me and the rest of his empire by catching me out again. I dreaded going to work in the mornings.

For weeks I fought this internal struggle. The residual fear of the nastier things I'd seen, balanced against the attraction of secret knowledge. The realisation I could follow in Grandad's footsteps, and the thought I'd passed up an opportunity to do real good. Creatures from nightmares, people bent and aged by exposure to magic, these thoughts kept me from deciding to join Mr Green and his colleagues in their mysterious world. But the longer I thought about it, the more I longed to find out more, and before too long I'd decided. I would get back in touch and see what they wanted from me, and what protection they had to offer. I convinced myself if I wasn't absolutely sure, I could still say no, but that it wouldn't hurt to ask.

One evening I sat in the living room with Green's slip of paper in one hand and a lit match in the other, trying to summon up the courage to put one to the other. When I did, the whole thing combusted in a green flash that left no smoke or ash. I sat there for a moment, blinking at the afterimages dancing in my eyes, wondering what happened next. Would Green walk out of the cupboard under the stairs? Or would his disembodied voice echo from one of the flower vases on the mantlepiece? The phone ringing jolted me from my thoughts. My annoyance at the interruption evaporated when I heard Mr Green's voice on the end of the line.

"Good evening, Mr Williams," he began. "I understand you'd like to talk to me?"

I stammered a response, trying to explain I wanted assurances on safety before I'd even consider it, but he shushed me.

"We can discuss it all over a nice civilised drink, Mr Williams. Will you join me in the Red Lion, in about 5 minutes?" he said, naming the local pub. I agreed, and the line went dead.

I found Green at the bar, two pints in front of him. As we drank, I noticed the strange silence fall over us as it had in the coffee shop on our first meeting, and I knew it prevented us being overheard. He spoke bluntly.

"You shouldn't have burnt the paper at home. I mentioned that magic can be traced," he said. "That was a minor charm, almost un-detectable. But if you return to work with us, then you will need to be a lot more careful in the future."

"That's what I wanted to talk to you about. I have a job already, do you pay people to work with you, or..." I took a sip of my beer to mask my embarrassment at bringing money into it.

"Oh, I'm afraid not, but we can arrange things such that your place of work believes you are on a long-term assignment and they continue to pay you. We find this is a much more economical way to operate," he smiled. "No-one will miss you."

"And I'd be safe?" I insisted.

"There are no guarantees in life, Mr Williams, you might have been hit by a bus on the way here tonight, might you not? I will say that you will be safer allied with us than not."

"What do you need me to do?"

He talked about their library of old case studies and research in need of digitisation, and the work my grandfather had done to refine their understanding of magic and the world of the Fae. By the end of our second pints I was excited about this new possibility. To my surprise, Mr Green agreed I should give it a trial for a few weeks and see what I could bring to the Society before deciding to stay. He urged me not to tell anyone about it, and to stick to the 'working for a remote client' line.

"Will I be commuting up to London, then?" I asked. "I suppose since your office is there, kind of, it'll be easier?" Green shook his head.

"We have a few routes to the Divide in this area, that's how I got here tonight."

"I don't suppose you'd set one up in the airing cupboard, that'd be convenient," I joked. His eyes flashed with anger.

"No!" he shouted, and even through the muting spell a few people turned to look. "That's a very dangerous idea," he continued. "Magic can be traced. Why do you fail to understand this? Putting it in your home would be the height of stupidity."

"I was just kidding, I heard you," I said. "I'll stick to the ones in town, hopefully no-one gets annoyed with me using all those 'employee only' doors all the time."

"You should vary your use of them, so no-one sees you using the same one too often." He wrote something on a piece of paper and smeared a pinkish powder from a short jar onto it. Passing it to me, I read the address of a nearby newsagent, and the words 'rear delivery door'. I looked up at him.

"For the time being, that paper will do the trick. Open the door with that wrapped around the handle, and it'll do the rest. Come in tomorrow morning, and we'll get you organised."

With that he rose and the buzz of the bar resumed around us. We shook hands again, and he walked over and entered the gent's toilets. When he didn't come back after a few minutes, I realised that he'd left the pub via that door, and no-one around had noticed.

The next morning the atomiser, pin and compact in my jacket pocket banged against my side as I snuck around the back of the newsagent's. I forced myself to look relaxed while I looked for the delivery door. It was locked, but I pulled the slip of paper from my wallet and placed it in my palm as I gripped the handle. I felt a light tickle in the palm of my hand and turned the handle. This time the door pulled open, and the dark corridor stretched in front of me. With one last glance over my shoulder, I stepped in and closed the door behind me. The gentle glowing blue light followed me as I made my way along the passageway with mounting excitement.

CHAPTER ELEVEN

AN UNPLEASANT REVELATION

A few metres up the corridor that disorienting wave of dizziness hit again, and then the white marble-tiled room coalesced around me. The ship-style door was closed in the wall, and I did not know how to open it. Tentatively I reached out for the wheel in the centre, but it spun of its own accord and the door swung open. Mr Green must have known I was coming as he stood in the reception area waiting. He extended his hand to me in greeting.

"Welcome back," he said. He led me along the corridor and stopped at the door we'd entered on my last visit, except now the gold lettering on the glass pane had changed:

Mr R. Brown
Research

"We thought you might as well have his old office, I think it's always best to keep things in the family," he said, as I opened the door and walked inside.

"This was my Grandad's office?" I said. He nodded. "But why Mr

Brown?"

"All in good time."

There were few changes in the office since my earlier tour. They had replaced the dead fern with a live one, emptied the wastepaper basket, and a sleek new laptop and a document scanner replaced the old typewriter. The giant window revealed a view of London in the fog. Today's forecast had been for sun and occasional rain showers, so I knew this wasn't London as it was today.

I couldn't see enough to work out what period in history I might have been observing until I looked up. A barrage balloon floated above me, tether lines vanishing into the mist.

"Must be the Blitz," Green mused. "If it's near dark, you might get a hell of a show."

"Are we safe? What if a bomb..."

"We're not really here, any more than we are anywhere. We can see London, but it cannot see or hurt us. It's fascinating, isn't it?"

I had to agree, but wasn't as excited as he was to watch London being bombed from the air. I wished the window had curtains I could draw over this view.

"The view might shift before then." Green sighed. "Anyhow, let's get you set up with the tools of the trade."

"You've sorted me out a computer at least," I said. "Is there somewhere to plug it in, though? There aren't any sockets."

"I think you'll find the battery life quite... surprising. But come, you can play with that later."

Green led me to a lab indistinguishable from the one I'd visited before, except for the sign on the door proclaiming it to be suitable for only Level One Containment. That suggested I shouldn't meet anything as terrifying this time.

The woman in the crisp white lab coat I'd met on my earlier visit joined us there, and he reminded me that her name was Ms Black. I caught myself staring at her.

"I feel like I'm in Reservoir Dogs, with all these colours," I joked to cover my embarrassment, and she smiled.

Mr Green sighed. "It's a necessary precaution. One of many you will need to adopt. Words have power, names even more so. Knowing and using someone's true name is a means of control, so we use pseudonyms to protect ourselves. You now have the name 'Brown', from your family's line."

"At least it's not Mr Pink." I smiled at Ms Black. "But is this all necessary?"

"Within these walls we are safe to be ourselves, but we use the pseudonyms wherever we are to avoid slipping up elsewhere. Let's equip you to travel as you please."

Ms Black produced a mahogany case the size of a hardback book. Brass clips held it closed, a brass hinge crossed the back and a leather strap let me hang it from my shoulder. It looked as old as anything I'd encountered here, but exquisite. I could picture it in an antique shop with an eye-watering price tag attached. She placed it on the desk, I unfastened the clips with a satisfying snap and opened it.

Inside the top half of the case, held in place with thin leather straps, were several tiny glass jars with cork stoppers. The lower half contained a small silver folding knife and a cheap plastic lighter which looked out of place among the antiques. There were empty spaces into which my compact, atomiser and silver pin fit perfectly. I secured them with the straps, snapping brass studs into place, and turned my attention to the jars in the top.

They were scratched, with their yellowing labels peeling off and unreadable, suggesting they'd been mouldering in the box for years. Half a dozen of them looked newer though, with clear glass and bright white paper labels. Each contained a quantity of powder and had the address of a location within my home town written in tiny copperplate handwriting. Ms Black explained that they would prime the Divide to take me there. "Make sure you vary the location at random, so no-one can predict where you might travel to and from," she reminded me. "And these," she said, pointing at a packet of cigarette papers, "will unlock routes to the Divide for you to come back here, until we can teach you how to do that yourself."

"You say your Society's purpose is to fight supernatural threats, but are there that many like that one I saw before? It must be hard to keep them under wraps if there are."

Mr Green nodded. "That's true, there are a number of different Fae and not all of them are so... cruel. But some will go after people or animals, I'm afraid. We trace a lot of missing cats and dogs to Fae attacks. Cats are sensitive to the frequencies they operate on, and when these creatures know something has seen them, they can often become aggressive. Once they get a taste for flesh, they're not too fussy where they get it, so people are at risk too. We locate threats and deal with them as best we can. That requires research such as your grandfather did, and development of spells to take the fight to them and protect ourselves. We have people here dedicated to each of these activities, and more besides. We hope you can improve our knowledge gathering and reveal some new insights we can use."

I looked at the mahogany case. "Was this my grandfather's too?"

"Yes, one of the things we recovered from the basement," Green said.

"He had lots of his research upstairs too, that's where I found the book."

Green sighed. "Yes, no doubt he didn't want to sit in the basement to compile his guide, but it would have been dangerous to do it out in the open. I suspect he thought his protections were sufficient, but he was wrong."

"Are you saying he didn't die from a heart attack? The certificate said..." If they had covered up a devastating fire, falsifying a death certificate wouldn't be difficult.

Black busied herself with the apparatus behind her. Mr Green could not meet my eye as he spoke. "I'm afraid your grandfather was attacked. He grew complacent and someone found him."

"Someone? Or something, like that thing you showed me? Why would they attack him?"

"Mostly, those creatures remain indifferent to our existence. They're drawn to magic like moths to a flame, with no agenda or understanding. However, they can be controlled, guided, used. Someone did precisely that and sent them after your grandfather."

Chapter Twelve

A Promising Beginning

My legs trembled as a surge of fear and anger poured into me. No matter how terrified I'd been of the creatures they'd showed me, part of me hadn't believed I was in mortal danger. Now I knew.

"Train me," I said. "Teach me how to fight, so I don't end up like he did."

"We had hoped to use your abilities in a more... academic role," Green said.

"Sod that," I said. "If whoever killed him is still a danger, then that's where I want to be. Show me how!"

"No."

"Why the hell not?"

"Let's discuss this somewhere more comfortable," he said. Without waiting for a reply, he walked out of the room, leaving me little choice but to scurry after him.

He led me along various corridors and stopped in to meet a few people he thought I might find helpful to know. All had gracious things to say about Grandad and expressed sadness at his passing. As we walked, Green explained more about his time at the Society.

"His father Jacob was one of our earliest members. He made some fundamental changes which put the Society on the path we follow today. And, as a result, he rose to high office. His son, your grandfather, followed in his footsteps and, while he never wished to run the Society, he still earned respect for his abilities, both magical and mundane. He put into place a few changes of his own. It's because of his work that we understand as much as we do about the Fae threat and have the information organised. The book you found was his greatest work. It explains so much and puts into a single volume everything we know about fighting back."

"So that can help me, teach me what I need."

Green sighed. "You're no match for what's out there. And before you ask again, training you would take too long. Not to mention that learning to control magic itself is dangerous. Maybe one day you'll be ready, but we need your help now. Believe me when I say that you can best avenge your grandfather by helping us in here."

"This isn't about revenge," I said.

"Yes, it is. And I'd be on the warpath in your situation. But trust me that the best thing you can do right now is inside this room," he said, gesturing to my office. We stepped inside, sat at opposite ends of a large green leather sofa, and he poured tea. Someone had brought in shelves of books and piles of boxes, which I recognised from the basement of my grandfather's house.

"So I'm to be your librarian?" I said. "It barely feels like I'll be able to make any difference at all."

"Don't underestimate the power of knowledge. Your grandfather collated a great deal of information already, but he hardly scratched the surface of our centuries of experience. If you can't make a breakthrough with all the tools and records we're placing at your disposal, then I've sorely misjudged you."

I had to admit he had a point. And part of me relished the challenge of finding the hidden gems of knowledge in a vast collection of information. I didn't want to take a back seat.

"OK," I conceded. "Let me see what I can do. But I still want to get more involved when the time comes."

"You have my word. If I believe you can help us in a more tangible way, you will be the first to know. But I should let you get settled in and make a start. We've transferred some of your grandfather's materials here for you to be getting on with. If there's anything else you need, then just give me or Janice at reception a call."

I was about to ask how, but he strode over to the desk and tapped a shallow bronze bowl etched with designs that twisted and writhed when I wasn't looking directly at them. He instructed me to grip either side with my hands and concentrate on the reception desk. I did so, and a thick black liquid resembling oil filled the bowl from nowhere, remaining level with the rim of the bowl no matter how I tilted it. The oil shimmered once and formed into a bas-relief of the woman who sat at reception. The image smiled and her lips moved as if speaking, but no sound came from the bowl. Instead, her words echoed in my head without passing through my ears. "Yes, Mr Brown, what can I do for you?" I almost dropped the bowl and stammered that I was just testing. "Call me any time if there's something you need," she replied, and the oil settled back to its flat blank state for a moment before draining away. I replaced the bowl on the desk and leaned back in the chair.

Green left, and the view of London outside caught my eye again. It took me a moment to realise what was wrong. Tower Bridge was still under construction if I looked along the river. When had that been built? Hold on, I thought, and turned my attention to the laptop. It appeared connected to the mains and charged despite a complete absence of power cables, a dim glow emanating from beneath it. I opened a web browser and it connected, allowing me to verify that Tower Bridge had opened on June 30th 1894, placing the view somewhat before that.

I had a magic laptop and a room full of books. The volumes were hand-bound, written by other members of the Society. Opening a couple at random I found them full of underlinings, highlighted sections, and crossings out, along with margin notes in Grandad's handwriting saying things like "No! Idiocy!" and "This might work." These must have been more of the source material for his own book, and he hadn't been shy about sharing his opinion of his predecessors' work.

The boxes contained his own research notes and rough draughts of his book. I paged through these more thoroughly, looking for somewhere logical to begin. The information he'd gathered was enormous in scope. I would need to continue as he'd begun, researching what they had already discovered and looking for links between sources. With a minor effort I configured a working database on the laptop ready to load the documents into, with rudimentary cross-referencing. When I added fresh material, it would look for phrases in common between sources, and flag them up for further review. I was confident I could train it to identify helpful things as I learned more myself, but for now a simple comparison would get things off the ground.

By the time I'd got the first book digitised and ready to go, I started by picking out keywords manually and letting the computer build from there. It would add more words as they came up in texts, but for now I'd steer it in the directions I wanted. I entered a few words I expected would be there: defence, spell, magic (and variant spellings), Fae (ditto), creature, monster, and set it working. Within moments it had cross-referenced the keywords to locations in each book, and I pulled up small sections of the text for each one to view its context. Now for a more tricky challenge, combining those words to do something useful. I started small with a search request: "defensive spells". The computer knew to look for those two words close together, and that 'spells' could swap with 'magic' (or magik, magics, magick etc.) and 'defensive' was just another form of 'defence' so it prepared me a list. The closer the words were found in the source material, the higher it ranked the result. I would get references like 'these are simple defensive spells, but effective' as a complete phrase at the top of the list, while 'a good approach when facing a magic user is always to consider your defences carefully' would come further down the page. Satisfied it was working, I moved on to the next book on the shelves.

After I'd worked through the top shelf of the bookcase, I had an excellent selection of data to play with in a more complex way. I decided to test by searching for texts that discussed the origins and nature of magic.

From piecing together the various sources the computer had ingested, I could learn a lot already. Magic was not part of nature, at least not part of the nature we understood. If you go back far enough, all of life on Earth stems from a common ancestor billions of years ago. What we call the Fae evolved from a unique source, one that was separate to our world. Beyond this the various sources diverged in opinion. Some spoke of other planes of existence, other dimensions, and one even tried to use quantum theory to explain it, but the upshot is that the Fae don't fit into our world. It's this which makes them undetectable to our senses, invisible and inaudible except under particular circumstances. Cats can see them, as Green had implied, as they were more sensitive to what the books called the 'Other Place'. So too were children and the mentally ill, or those under great stress.

The Fae and the magic they embodied had developed together. This gave them a much greater ability to manipulate magic than humanity ever could. And, it appeared, a greater ability to tolerate the effects it had on the mind.

Magic allows us to bridge the gap between their places and ours, it brings the Other World close. That has numerous effects which concerned the Society. First, it weakens the space between worlds so things can come through. Second, glimpses of that Other Place tend to badly affect the magic user. Each book again had a different opinion on why this happened, as everyone who'd seen it has a unique way of explaining what they saw. Where their reports converged were that it is just 'wrong' in every way. The geometry doesn't work as we are used to, eyes twist as if looking at an optical illusion. The creatures were unnerving, the sounds disorienting. Even the shortest exposure to their world would unnerve you, and the more you used magic the more exposure. I might imagine someone getting used to it over time, but the books explained that the initial impression of strangeness never fades and always takes a toll on the mind. Some people are stronger than others and keep their faculties for years. Others find it overwhelms them on a first viewing. And there was no way to tell in advance which group someone will find themselves in.

I shuddered. If any exposure to magic was be so terrifying, so disorienting, was I in danger from my experience so far? I switched my search focus to the human impact of magical experimentation. To my dismay, I found dozens of results in every book I'd scanned, and my grandfather's notes were at the top. I clicked on the link and read carefully, my pulse racing.

His words spoke of a colleague of his, the strongest magic user in generations. She could gaze into the Other Place for hours on end and not suffer so much as a headache. She managed spells he had believed impossible, fought the greatest perils, and appeared immune to the effects he expected.

But she wasn't.

She grew addicted to the extra power she was developing, but hid it well. By the time my grandfather realised, she was too far gone. The only saving grace was that her mind was intact, so he could reason with her, convince her to give it up. And she tried, she truly did. But he had underestimated its hold on her and the damage it had done. One night she sensed something calling from between the worlds. In her weakened state, she wasn't able to resist taking a peek to see what or who it was calling to her. That attracted even more attention from Beyond and whatever was There, it called to her again. She went through to the other place. To the land of the Fae.

Chapter Thirteen

A Terrible History

It had long been theorised that it was impossible for us to travel there, and that even if it were achieved it'd be fatal to us. However, a few weeks later the Society got signs that she'd come back. They'd been monitoring the usual weak spots when they detected something powerful come through. Green dispatched teams to investigate, but they never returned. When another group was sent to check on them they found only one man alive. He said it had been her, back from the Other Place. She was insane and blamed the Society for everything that had happened to her. He said she'd vowed revenge against every one of them.

I stepped away from the computer and stretched to release the knots in my spine. This woman, unnamed in the books, must be the adversary the Society was fighting, the person Green had implied was behind my grandfather's death. I used the bowl on my desk to call him and ask. He listened as I explained what I'd found and promised to be right over to see me.

I realised I didn't know how to order the tea, which had always been waiting for Mr Green when he wanted it. I used the dish again to ask Janice, who said she'd send it along right away. While I waited, I searched the web for the state-of-the art in natural language pattern matching and downloaded 'proof of concept' programs to test against my database.

A knock on the door announced the arrival of my tea, and I called out for the bearer to come in. The door opened and a figure three-and-a-half feet tall carried in a tray with a teapot, cups and saucers. The creature was stick-thin, with jet-black eyes and hair and pointed ears. It smiled, pointed teeth glinting in a wide slash of a mouth. It was naked apart from a loincloth, and its skin was pure white. Hoofed feet clattered on the floor as it walked over to the table. I sat frozen in place as it gently deposited the tray on the table with long thin fingers, sharp-looking nails clattering on the surface. It turned to face me, bowed deep, and walked out of the room. I was still staring after it when Mr Green arrived.

"I see you met Marlin," he said as he sat on the sofa. "One of the few Fae that seems to like humans. He came to stay with us many years ago and makes himself useful. Milk?"

I sipped hot tea as Mr Green explained. While most Fae were in-different to humanity, drawn towards us only if we used magic, there were those that were more curious. "In fact, I have heard tell that there is an equivalent to our Society Over There researching us," he said. Members of the Society had captured Marlin years earlier, and he had agreed to share information in return for 'kinder treatment'. When I asked Green outright if they used torture, he explained that most of the creatures they encountered never hesitated to do much worse to us. I protested, while remembering I'd been prepared to destroy the caged beast that had been following me. That had been a dumb and dangerous animal, I reasoned, not a sentient creature as Marlin was.

"They tortured Marlin," I said, "and to stop it he agreed to come here and be... what, a tea boy?" I asked. "You said he shared information, why isn't he doing research?"

"We learned all we could. His knowledge is far from complete, so we're always hoping for someone else to come over." Green explained that Over There was similar to here, in one respect. Distinct parts of their world had unique creatures, just as ours did. He opened a substantial book he'd brought with him and quoted:

"For just as nature in all her diversity has filled this Earth with wonders, so she has that one. And all the variety of our world can find a mirror — after all, the lion and the elephant are unique to Africa, should not the same be true of the Fae?"

"What's the book?" I asked.

"A copy of your grandfather's work, we thought you might like it. We should keep the original safe, but we had our scribes make copies for certain key members, and I asked for one for you too."

I ignored his implication and opened the book. It was beautifully copied by hand from Grandad's original. I would have my work cut out bringing this lot into the 20th Century, let alone the 21st. I got back to the subject that was preying on my mind.

"I wanted to ask about this woman, who travelled over to the Fae world."

"Olivia Fallowes, yes. The brightest and best of her generation."

"My grandfather said she became addicted. Why do magic at all if it's so dangerous?" I asked. "You don't want to bring the spaces closer, bring those things over here, so why take the risk?"

"Indeed. But some locations are already weak. Most reports of haunted houses are places with weak points. Generations ago people built stone circles to contain weaknesses, but while they protect us they also make the space inside the circle weaker. Since things are coming through anyhow, we need to work magic to combat them. Fortunately, the wounds we create can heal if they're left alone. We cannot say the same for the people who use magic. It has a cost. I told you that before, but I didn't explain."

"She went insane, I read."

"Yes, it can have very serious mental effects. And that's not the only way magic extracts its price. It can also have some rather extreme physical effects, too."

"That woman who locked the door in the lab. She looked used up, worn out. And that lesson tired me out. But I feel fine now, and I saw nothing unusual other than that creature. No glimpses of another world."

"You would feel fine after a cigarette or two. Smoke twenty a day for life and you'd soon not. Some folks only get a cough, while some develop emphysema, lung cancer or heart disease. You can't predict what happens to whom, but you increase the odds of something nasty with every puff. Magic is similar. There are no significant risks from the odd minor spell now and again, you'll barely notice the effects. But something big is very different. Chain-smoke a box of cigars and you'll suffer more than just enjoying one. Do that every day and you cause permanent damage."

"Why are people willing to use magic, with those risks?"

"It's addictive. The cigarette analogy still holds, smoking kills you and costs a fortune, yet people can't stop themselves. You remember how euphoric you were with that power coursing through you? Imagine that a hundred-fold, you'd soon find you didn't mind the lows as long as the highs kept coming."

I recalled the intense experience and understood what he meant.

"If you've ever been or met an addict, you appreciate that at some point all that matters is the next fix. No matter what they have to do to get it, they'll do it. Steal, beg, borrow or even kill. Going cold turkey from magic is agony: you're exhausted all the time, and often you can still see glimpses of the Other Place out of the corner of your eye, hear it calling you. If your mind is already weak, withdrawal is unbearable. And so people relapse, each new spell damaging their fragile hold on reality still further. We monitor our people as best we can, but addicts are good at hiding the signs. If we fail, we can only try to contain them instead."

"And the person you're fighting, this happened to them. And you think she's responsible for what happened to my grandfather?"

He nodded and sipped his tea. "We've not seen her in a while, but we believe she's behind several recent attacks. They've been more organised, more focused than the usual Fae activity, as if someone was guiding them."

Olivia Fallowes. "You used her actual name!" I realised.

"We have no interest in protecting her now, and to be frank we can use any power we can gain over her. There's no point in referring to her as 'Mrs Green' any longer."

Chapter Fourteen

A Practical Application

"Yes," he confirmed, "she was my wife. And until she turned from us, the love of my life." He sighed. "Now, I'm afraid, she isn't even truly human. I've long had to consider her dead, but my grief still lingers." He wiped a slight tear from his eye and stood. I tried to express my sorrow, but he waved me aside. "Shouldn't you be getting home?" he said.

I realised it was 7pm. Time to put the travel kit they had given me to the test.

The first glass vial from the mahogany case allowed me to use the Divide to travel home, and I emerged from the rear door of the local kebab place moments later. As I walked home, I sensed I was being followed, but couldn't see anything despite frequent checks over my shoulder.

In no time, I exhausted the supply of books in my office. With the help of the Scry (as I discovered the bowl for communication was called) I could ask for information from the Society's capacious archives to get new raw material. I began working on digitising field reports to track incidents over time and seeking patterns in Fae activity, and Marlin delivered piles of boxes to me each morning and removed them again at night. His regular visits soon turned into chances to talk to him, and during one of these I asked him about his life in the Society.

"I enjoy my work," he said, his voice thin and dry like crackling leaves.

"Yes, but there's more to life than work," I pressed. "What do you do in your spare time?"

He paused in loading his cart with boxes for a moment. "I watch movies."

"That's it? You don't go outside?"

"I am not permitted. I would 'frighten the natives', Mr Green says."

"So you're stuck inside, like some sort of house-elf?"

He bristled, every hair on his head standing upright. "Please don't call me that. I have seen *Harry Potter*, and I was not amused."

"Oh I'm sorry, I didn't mean to offend you. I guess fantasy movies don't get everything right, do they?"

"I wouldn't know, I prefer romantic comedies," Marlin said as he left.

After a couple of weeks of research, Mr Green informed me he had teams working to prove the connections my programs had found, and to develop new and improved magical techniques based on my discoveries.

I asked if I might see this research. What little magic I'd encountered had been fascinating, if terrifying, and I was keen to witness the fruits of my labours being turned into something more tangible.

Green was reluctant. "Your work is proving invaluable, I don't wish you to become distracted," he said. "The deeper you dig into the books, the more insightful your discoveries are."

"It wouldn't take long. And you said I'd be able to get involved more," I protested.

"If I felt it was appropriate," he replied. "We have enough going on already without me needing to worry about you. You're safer and more useful right where you are."

I pressed the point. "It's impossible to understand what you're looking for without some practical knowledge," I explained, "and if I can't do a decent job I don't want to do one at all. You keep telling me that what I'm doing is valuable. I'm telling you I can't do it without your agreement."

He pondered this for a moment. "Very well, but just to observe. I really can't have you pulled away from your studies for too long."

He was as good as his word. Within the week he called me on the Scry to invite me to a demonstration in one of the labs, where we found Tina Black packing things wrapped in newspaper into a cardboard box.

"How are you settling in?" she asked. "Pretty well, judging by the material Mr Green here has been bringing me. It seems you're able to spot connections the rest of us have missed!" I tried to explain that it was the computer's work and asked what she had managed so far.

"Ah, this is exciting," she said. "Your idea that the spray we used to make the Fae visible in our world and the historical use of 'hag stones' might be linked in some underlying way, got us into a new area of research."

If I'd been able to get a word in edgeways, I would have asked what a hag stone was. My computer might have 'read' those books, but I hadn't. Ms Black noticed the flicker in my eyes and gave me a wink.

"*As you know*, hag stones let the user see Fae that have come over here. They have to be made of a special rock which has a naturally formed viewing hole through the centre. It's no good drilling one out by hand as it just won't work. That means they're rather rare, so we only have a few in our arsenal here. Plus, you're not all that subtle walking around with a donut shaped rock held to your eye.

"Hence we use the sprays, which are easier to make. But as you saw, the effect of the spray is short lived and renders the creature visible to everyone. Not something we want to encourage, if we're trying to remain undetected ourselves. It also tells the Fae themselves they've been spotted. A spray in the face is not stealthy!"

Green interjected. "I've been caught out that way myself, you just try to convince someone you're spraying for rats when an imp flashes into existence in front of them and starts shouting at you."

"Right. Your discovery let us look for common characteristics, and we took some scrapings from a hag stone and discovered that the ore it's made from contains several of the same elements as the spray. This led us to experiment further with which were essential and which were not, something I've been asking to do for a long time." She glanced at Mr Green, who ignored her. "And I narrowed it down to a particular combination of chemicals in the right proportions influencing the wavelengths of the light. It's not all science, there's still some magic involved, but the result is..." She paused for effect before whipping a black cloth off a small tray on the bench top. "Ta-dah!"

"Glasses?"

"Glasses," she agreed, "which can reveal the hidden world around us!" With that, she handed a pair each to Mr Green and I, and slipped on the third pair herself. I removed my regular glasses and replaced them with the new ones, thick tortoiseshell frames and heavy glass which slid down my nose if I glanced downwards. "They're all we had in the stores," Ms Black apologised. "I can treat your own glasses if you'd prefer, then you'll be ready any time."

I squinted around the lab. Nothing appeared different. Ms Black opened a small box that sat on the floor beside the bench and pulled out an old coffee jar with holes punched into the lid. Inside sat an angry looking rat-like creature with no tail. When it opened its mouth, its incisors sat where the canine teeth should be. It put me in mind of a vampire, an idea strengthened by its front feet reminiscent of hands, agile fingers grasping at the inside of the jar to find a way out. It had intelligent eyes, and it fixed me with a beady glare before going back to scratching its long teeth against the glass.

I lifted the glasses, and she was holding an empty jar. Dropping the lenses back over my eyes, the creature came back into view. "That's re-markable!" I said. "We can discover anything unusual with no trouble at all!"

Ms Black shifted uneasily. "There are some drawbacks," she admitted. "If you go outside, you catch glimpses of the Other Side from time to time. You can't see it in here since we're shielded magically, but away from our warding, it's risky. It'd be better not to wear them all the time," she suggested. I agreed, peering at the rat-thing in the jar. Everything about it made my skin crawl.

"Thank you, Ms Black," Mr Green said. "How many have you prepared so far? We can get them into the field right away."

"About ten pairs so far, but if you can get me some set for people's prescriptions I can do another ten this week."

"I can't hear it," I said. "It's scratching away at that glass, but it's not making a noise!"

"No, glasses work on light, not sound," Ms Black explained.

"But those things I saw before, that big thing and the one I used magic on, I heard them all right." I couldn't forget the pained howl, or the scratch of feet on the cage floor.

"Yes, the spray is the only way of hearing them unless we set them."

"Set them? What does that mean?"

"Make them permanently visible, like we did to that Chivato."

"That's its name? Chivato?"

Green interrupted my quick fire questions. "We have to give them names to keep track of them, and we pick something from mythology that we think fits. Or that sounds 'cool'." He aimed this last at Ms Black who muttered under her breath that it was important that names sounded right.

"I should get back," I said as I swapped the magical lenses over for my own glasses. "But thanks for the demonstration, that was 'cool'!" Green rolled his eyes as Ms Black and I traded grins.

"Come back any time, I have a few other things I can show you."

Green and I left the lab and headed back up the corridor towards my office. "I hope that helped you to see the value of your work. Those glasses alone will be an enormous benefit."

"It sounded as if you needed them urgently, is something going on? Is Olivia attacking?"

"She has stepped up the attacks, it's true. But we have matters in hand, I assure you. Please don't trouble yourself."

"I'm willing to learn, you know. If I can pick up some magic..."

"No, that will not be happening," Green snapped. "We discussed the dangers of magic recently, surely you understand that it would be far too risky to let you experiment with it."

"Then teach me, or let someone else do it. They can monitor me, make sure I'm not losing control."

"No," he said. "And that's the end of the matter."

CHAPTER FIFTEEN

A STARTLING SIGHT

Green's refusal to allow me to learn more stung me, and for a few days I threw myself into my research in an effort to understand about magic despite him. I soon discovered that while the books were a fascinating insight into the Society's history and magic's place in the world, they were terrible for learning anything practical. Even the most explicit references to performing a specific spell were still too vague to follow, and my efforts to do even the simplest were fruitless. I found that I was unable to reproduce the shield spell I'd learned on my first visit.

While my cross-referencing was producing new insights, I still knew that I could better focus my efforts if I understood the uses to which the Society would put it. Tina had extended me what I took to be an open invitation, so I arranged to meet her in her lab for another demonstration.

I couldn't hide my disappointment at the uninteresting projects she had to show me. "Don't you have anything more exciting?" I asked. "Perhaps something that you would use in the field? Weapons maybe, or even protective amulets?"

"I don't get to work on the good stuff," she said. "And I don't get into the field either. But if you want a pocket-sized Scry, or a rain-repelling hat, I'm your girl."

"Aren't all hats rain-repelling?"

"This one keeps your entire body dry and warm, no matter the weather, but yeah it's not exactly earth-shattering."

"I'm sorry. Mind you, it's hardly thrilling scanning in books and files all day, either."

"It's infuriating, we're smart people and they won't use us to our full abilities." She paused for a moment. "I know why they won't promote me, I don't 'fit in'. But you're one of the boys."

"Not that it's doing me much good, I almost had to fight Green to get to see you."

"Oh, that's sweet." She smiled. "I don't have many visitors, let alone those who'd fight for me!" There was a twinkle in her eye, and I realised this was the first time someone had flirted with me in years. I elected not to tell her it was the magic I'd really wanted to see. "But you have some talent, I noticed that in our first encounter, so I think you should be prepared to use it."

"I agree!" I said. "Sadly you and I are the only ones who think that way. Mr Green forbade me from learning anything, I think he's scared I'd go rogue."

Tina scoffed. "It's not likely," she said. "I mean sure, it happens, but there're warning signs and it's been a long time since someone lost control. I'd start you off with some simple things, basic defences and the like."

"You'd be willing to teach me?" I asked.

"If Green's forbidden it, I really shouldn't," she said. "Oh, don't give me the sad puppy eyes. I'm not saying I won't, just that we need to be very careful. Both to make sure you don't go off the deep end and to make sure no-one finds out. What do you say to a couple of hours a day?"

"That'd be fantastic! But how can we keep it quiet? If I'm not in my office, people will notice, and it'll not be long before they find out I'm down here..."

"We'll say you're helping me with my research, and I'm helping with yours. In the current situation, no-one will argue since they're pushing for results. And if anyone suspects we're having an affair, then they'd be expecting us to sneak around and lie about it, so that works out perfectly!" she giggled.

I smiled despite myself. "You know I'm still technically married, right?"

"I don't think learning magic counts as cheating, silly. Shall we get started?" She showed me a cage containing a half-dozen white mice. "Don't worry, what I'll teach you today will work on them just the same, and this way I needn't sign out anything more exotic from the Vaults. Let's start with a refresher of that barrier you created last time."

"Will it hurt them?" I asked, watching the mice playing and tumbling in their cage.

"No. That spell creates the sensation of pain and discomfort to urge the target away from someone, it doesn't do any actual harm."

"Won't I need those pills again?" I asked. "I've not had much luck practising on my own."

"Probably not. They unlocked your latent ability, so you might be ready to tap into it without help this time. Plus, you have me helping you out! Now relax, breathe deep and conjure up that power."

It took a few minutes of meditative breathing and Tina's guidance before I sensed the familiar rising power inside me. The exhilaration was overwhelming as I stretched my arms out towards the mice in the cage, my hands rising and falling in time with the energy within me, and took a deep breath.

"Don't hold your breath!" she called, and I lost focus. Breathing deeply, I rebuilt the waves until they reached a peak even higher than before. I created the bubble around myself and experimented with increasing its size towards the cage. Unlike the Fae I'd worked with before, the mice showed no sign of distress, but they still moved away as it approached.

I found the control grew easier the longer I practised, but when I turned to tell her this, so did the force of the barrier I'd erected. All the lab equipment on the desks flew and shattered against the walls. Stools tumbled over and Tina let out an agonised scream as my barrier washed over her, knocking her to the floor. The bubble surrounding me burst as I ran forward to where she'd fallen.

She was lying immobile, but lifted her head and groaned as I knelt beside her. She flashed a wry smile for a second before she grimaced in pain again. "Are you OK?" I asked, as I tried to help her to her feet. I could barely raise her to a sitting position. I was drained, as if I'd not slept in days and then run a marathon. I flopped on the floor next to her, and leaned against the bench behind me, my head throbbing.

"It's OK, I'll live," she groaned, and leant against me for a while, catching her breath as I stammered apologies and explanations. "Don't worry, I should have warned you that you might have caught me with it, but your enthusiasm was rather contagious," she reassured me.

"It sounded like I hurt you, are you sure you're not injured?"

She shook her head. "Rather than my approaching you slowly and experiencing the urge to retreat, you smacked me full on so the effect was rather... intense." I swallowed hard and apologised again. She nodded towards a stool nearby, and I picked it up and helped her onto it with difficulty. My left hand was as numb as if I'd lain asleep on it all night. I shook my hand to kick life back into my fingers, but it didn't help.

She took my hand in hers, drifting her fingers across my palm and along the fingers of my numbed hand. The sensations returned with a rush and she opened her eyes and smiled at me. I blushed.

"Thanks," I muttered. "Will it always affect me like that?"

"Not as long as you keep control. You collapsed the bubble when you panicked, so the magic dissipated. If you re-absorb the energies, it won't drain you like that. Offensive spells use up the power and can't be recovered, so they'll take more out of you."

"But you just put more energy into me, to heal me. Won't that hurt you then?" I asked. "You were weak enough already."

"I only topped you up. You'd have recovered in time anyhow, but now we can share the load. We heal a portion each, instead of you having to do it all."

"Could I just take power from someone, if I needed it? If you can give it to me freely, what stops me just taking it?"

"Don't even joke about that," she snapped, dropping my hand. "That's a sure sign of someone losing their grip on magic, when they go around stealing it. It comes at too high a price to be worthwhile, and besides, it's incredibly dangerous. You have to rip it out of someone's body, and that has many horrific side effects." I mumbled an apology, and she softened. "It's an obvious question, we're just rather sensitive to it around here."

I tried a joke. "I'll add it to the list of things we don't tell anyone, I guess!" and felt relief at Tina's smile.

I regretted taking this exit from the Divide. My choice had been on the far side of a park behind the town, but I'd forgotten that it was long after sunset. A thickening mist had gathered, reducing visibility to mere yards. Dim sodium lighting only illuminated a tiny sickly circle around each streetlamp and cast thick dark shadows between them. I'd welcomed the walk as a chance to stretch my legs and clear my mind, but my tired brain filled every shadow with a lurking menace. Some formed monstrous, demonic creatures watching my too-slow progress, and others looked almost human, which were even more terrifying. When a figure that loomed out of the thickening fog turned out to be real rather than imagined, my overwrought imagination caused my heart to leap into my throat.

"Good evening," the dog walker called to me, and my voice croaked as I returned the greeting. I glanced back over my shoulder as he vanished back into the mist behind me, and the last thing I saw were his dog's eyes reflecting the yellow of the street light above me.

A sudden squeak to my left made me jump again, nausea rising along with the panic. I made out a child's swing rocking back and forth on its chains, but could not tell what had started it swaying. There was no breeze to stir it, and nobody nearby. At least, nothing visible.

I ran. All efforts to calm myself, to remind myself that I was safe were for nothing and my feet pounded on the pavement until I reached my front door. I struggled to unlock the door, every second fumbling with the keys believing something was preparing to grab me from behind. After an eternity, I unlocked the door, fell through and slammed it behind me. I then turned into the kitchen and vomited into the sink.

"Oh my God!"

The terror still filling my body, I jumped at the sound of a voice behind me.

Chapter Sixteen

A Rising Panic

I relaxed as I recognised Claire, and she got me a glass of water to rinse my mouth. I mumbled something about going out after work for a quick bite to eat and it must have disagreed with me, while still fighting to catch my breath and slow my heartbeat.

She led me through to the living room, lay me on the sofa and covered me with a blanket. "Why are you here?" I asked.

"You're welcome," she snapped.

"Sorry, thank you, you're an angel. Why are you here?"

She looked at her feet. "I thought someone was following me," she said. "I realised I was nearby and thought you might help. Luckily I still have my key, since you were out drinking."

"I told you, it's food poisoning," I protested. "Who was following you?"

"I didn't see them, not in the fog. It was more a feeling, you know?" I did. If she'd had the same experience that I had, did that mean it was real? Was someone or something out there stalking me, or us? "What's that look for, did you see something too?" she asked.

"No. I felt dreadful so I barely paid attention to anything," I lied. "The fog always makes everything seem spooky though, it was probably just that."

"Don't patronise me, I was terrified."

"I can tell, you look almost as rough as I feel. Do you want to stay here tonight?" I asked. She frowned. "I didn't mean... You take the bed, I'll sleep here on the sofa."

I woke to the smell of toast and coffee. Claire stuck her head round the door, clutching her breakfast.

"Morning sleepyhead," she said. "There's a pot of coffee in there if you want some. How's the stomach?"

I sat up on the sofa. "Better, thanks. You feeling OK?"

"What, because I made you coffee?" She frowned at me over her cup.

"I meant after that fright last night," I said. "You seemed pretty rattled."

She took a bite of toast, chewed and swallowed it before answering. "Like you said, it was probably just the fog." Her knuckles were white around the handle of her mug.

"Stay here today if you like," I told her. "I know how a fright like that can linger." She visibly relaxed at the idea. "Will you be OK if I go to work though?"

"Yes, off you go. I'll see you later." As I went upstairs to shower and change, she called up after me. "Don't expect me to do your laundry though!"

My own fears of the night before evaporated in the morning sunshine, and by the time I reached the office I decided not to mention my paranoia to anyone. I had a special reason to want to get to work that day. I would be having my first lesson in the technique of remote viewing.

At its basic level, remote viewing worked by collecting light from one location by magical means and transferring it to another, much as a fibre-optic cable carries light along its length over hundreds of miles. This allows the magic user to view something happening miles away, potentially on the other side of the world.

"But let's not run before we can walk," Tina said. "We'll start with something more local." She tapped a box on the desk. "Inside here are five items, which I want you to identify without opening the box. Gather your energies and repeat these words after me." I collected my magical force and held it in my core, enough to hold the tingle inside my chest. I signalled I was ready, and Tina began speaking.

As I repeated the words, the memory of the sounds escaped. Imagine overhearing a conversation in a foreign language, but the words are quiet and you pick out nonsense phrases that sound sensible. As I spoke, the surrounding air shifted. A dull glow stretched between me and the box, while the rest of the room faded as if the lights had dimmed. The glow touched the front of the wooden box, passed inside and shone on the contents. I directed the light onto each item.

"There's a pack of playing cards," I said, "and... an apple?" Tina nodded. "I'm not sure, some sort of jar, I think..." The light burst brighter than ever and everything vanished into white. A figure stood in front of me, silhouetted against the blinding light, and walked towards me from a great distance. Each step brought them much closer than it should have, and they covered the vast distance in a few paces. As the figure reached me, the light softened and wrapped around it,

revealing the figure of a woman. She was old, tired-looking and wrinkled, grey hair sticking in all directions, with a glint in her eyes. Those
eyes though — they were jet-black marbles in her white face, no iris,
no whites, no hint of anything other than infinite, terrifying depths.
She reached her crooked arm towards me and touched my shoulder,
though I didn't feel it. Her cracked lips opened, and a whisper croaked
out.

"I have her."

She released my shoulder, turned and walked away, vanishing into
the light in a few paces. I sagged onto the edge of the desk in complete
exhaustion. Tina was at my side asking what happened. "You froze,
you looked terrified for a moment there. There was nothing in the box
to scare you. I mean, I considered putting a spider in there as a joke,
but..." she tailed off as I turned to face her. "You look like you've seen
a ghost," she breathed.

"Olivia," I whispered. I was sure it had been her. Who else would
have, could have, showed up in that way? And with a heart-sinking
certainty, I recognised what she was talking about.

"She's taken my wife."

I paced the lab, stabbing at my phone as if I could conjure up a signal.
Tina probed me for more details, not understanding how I realised it
was Olivia. I couldn't explain my absolute certainty, how the knowledge of both her identity and the meaning of her words had arrived
in my mind, but I wanted to run straight out of there and go to find

Claire.

"Even if you're right about who it was," she said, "she might be lying. And if she does have your wife, I'm sure it'll be a trap. Neither of us can deal with her alone, we need backup."

"What the hell else can I do?" I argued. "We can't go to Green with this. He didn't want me doing magic. For all I know, this is why!"

"We have to, though. I'm sure under the circumstances he won't argue about this."

"Then what?" I asked. "Even he's not ready to confront her, if the rumours you've been telling me about her are true... We just sit here and wait? No way."

"OK, OK," she agreed. "So we won't wait. But we have to believe Green will know what to do."

I didn't knock on the door of Green's office but walked straight in. He looked up from his work in irritation, but any protest died on his lips at the sight of our expressions.

"What's happened?" he asked, resignation in his voice. I blurted out what Olivia had told me, then sank into a chair, shaking.

I'd not explained it well. Green thought I'd met Olivia face-to-face and was more concerned with how I'd got away from her, until Tina explained it was a vision, brought on by our magical practice. His jaw clenched, his brow furrowed, but he remained silent.

In a few moments, Tina had explained everything. Green picked up his Scry and made a brief call I would have given anything to overhear.

This done, he spoke to us in a calm voice.

"We'll check, but I'm sure everything is fine. Mr Blue will contact our people who were watching your house." So they had been watching me. Was that who I'd sensed, what Claire had suspected last night? Or had it been Olivia? "If Olivia had turned up, they'd have reported it, so I think we'll have put your concerns to rest in a moment." At that, the brass Scry on his desk let out a low chime. He grasped the bowl in both hands, and his face dropped. My heart leapt into my throat.

In a voice barely audible, Green said, "The Watchers are dead."

I leapt back to my feet, ready to charge out of there, but he stopped me with a word. He explained that Blue was mobilising the best people to handle this threat, and to let him take care of things. I hurried after him as he sped toward the Divide.

"I'm coming with you," I said.

"Out of the question," he snapped. "You don't think you've done enough already? If you storm in there, we can't tell what might happen. You're a liability!"

"Nonsense, I didn't cause this!" I shouted. "Olivia didn't get to her because I was learning a few spells."

"Oh, so the vision was a coincidence? You've been practising magic, pushing against the barrier between worlds and she noticed. The best you can do now is to keep your damn head down and let the professionals sort out the mess you've created."

I looked over at Tina, but she dodged my gaze. "Please," I begged. "I have to know what's happened, if it's all true." The tears couldn't be held back any longer. "I have to."

"All right," he answered after a painful pause. "After Blue checks the place out."

The wait was endless. My mind offered me endless scenarios to ponder, each worse than the last. I was so lost in my thoughts that when a soft chime came from the pocket of Green's jacket I almost missed it. He pulled out a small dish which filled with a black liquid, a portable version of the Scry. He held a short, silent conversation with someone before turning to me.

"The house is empty." Green sighed. "There's no evidence of a struggle, no reason to be alarmed."

"What about the Watchers?" I asked. "You said they were dead, that sounds like reason enough."

"Even if it was her, it might just be another of her random attacks."

"She just happened to attack the people watching my house? I don't believe that, and I don't think you do either. But let's go then, put my mind at rest," I urged.

Exiting from a small door behind a cafe near my house, I tried calling Claire on my mobile. She didn't reply, it just rang until her voicemail picked up. I led the way home at a near run. Mr Blue stood outside the front door, while in front of the bushes across the road an elderly woman was making strange gestures. A shimmer passed over the foliage; she was masking the area from view. That must have been where the Watchers had been hiding.

Inside, the silence was oppressive. I dashed from room to room calling Claire's name. Maybe she'd just gone out? I felt dizzy as I saw her key hanging on the hook beside the door. Her purse, handbag and phone sat on the coffee table, as did one of Grandad's old leather-bound books. Something was sticking out from between the pages, like a bookmark. It was a simple white envelope of thick paper, unmarked, unlabelled and thick enough to obscure whatever was inside it. The flap wasn't sealed, and I pulled out a thick black piece of card the size of a postcard. It was blank.

The door opened. Tina stood there, unsure whether she should come in. I gestured to her, and she walked over, closing the door behind her.

"What's that?" she asked, as my gaze returned to the small card in my hand.

"I've no idea, just found it in a book," I replied, holding it up to show her.

"Put it down!" she cried. I turned over the card to see what had startled her, an intricate silver symbol embossed in foil. As soon as I saw it, the sigil turned to smoke and rose from the card into my face. It burned my throat as the smoke twisted in the air and dived into my mouth and nose.

Chapter Seventeen
An Important Message

If my house had been quiet before, the silence now was overwhelming. You don't notice the sounds that pervade your daily life until they're gone. I was no longer hearing the hum of the fridge, the occasional swish of cars on the road outside, even the soft tap from the airlock in the radiator I'd been meaning to look at. The silence was so total, so oppressive, that I wanted to shout just to break it, but that was nothing compared to the blackness that filled my eyes.

As a child I'd been into a cave complex on a family holiday in Wales, one of the rare ones where Dad had been there too. The guide told us we were too far underground for light to penetrate. To prove it he switched off the light, and we laughed to be plunged into darkness in such unfamiliar surroundings. He explained how your eyes can adjust to the tiniest sliver of light, that your house could never be this dark. Even a moonless night was never as black as you imagined, but no matter how long you waited down here, you'd never be able to see a thing. It didn't take long for the laughing to stop. The odd solitary voice called out 'echo' to hear their words reflected, and an occasional cough bounced like a gunshot off the surrounding walls. Before long we were all shifting uncomfortably, and I was blinking hard, certain my eyes had stopped working. No one wanted to be the first to ask for the lights, hoping that someone else would break. With an eye-watering flash, the lights had come back on, and a spattering of applause defused the tension.

I was blinking again now, I couldn't tell if my eyes were open or closed. Could Tina still see me, or was she blind too? I called out her name, but the sound died on my lips. I couldn't even hear my voice inside my head. I tried to touch my mouth to see if it moved when I spoke, but I didn't have any arms to move. I couldn't walk, couldn't move, couldn't sense my body. I was a disembodied mind, floating in black silence.

Time lost all meaning. I have no idea how long I drifted, scared and alone, before an imperceptible glow in front of me grew ever brighter, taking the rough outline of a person. As it brightened, details emerged, the first hints of a face, of hair, of clothes. The impression was that of a marble block gradually being carved into a bust. I don't recall when I first recognised the figure before me, but it stopped being the mere suggestion of a human and became a passable reproduction of my grandfather's face.

I had to wait another unknowable time before realising that he was moving, his head drooping before he gathered his thoughts and stared me right in the eyes.

"This will be difficult for you," he said. If I'd had eyes at that moment, I would have cried. "I didn't want you caught up in all of this, but if you're seeing this now, then I'm afraid the worst has happened. I don't know how much longer I have, but I've trusted this message to a friend who will get it to you if it should become necessary."

"Who?" I asked, but no sound came.

"By now you will have learned of my secret life, the life that should have been your father's and then yours, before he and your mother chose different paths. There are terrible threats to this world, and terrible people on both sides who will stop at nothing to make sure they get their way. Some of them must have caught up with me, or I'd be giving you this message in person. I would pray that you are safe, but if the past years have taught me anything, it's that God either doesn't exist or doesn't care a damn about the prayers of His people. There is a war going on, and you need to pick a side. It's not as simple as 'good' versus 'evil', 'light' versus 'dark'. Terrible things are done with righteous certainty, and yet more awful deeds come wrapped in the veil of the 'greater good'. You must listen to your conscience, choose with your heart, and decide what is right for yourself. I will tell you what I decided, and why I chose the path I did, despite the danger it's put me into. I ask you to listen to me carefully, and not to repeat anything you hear from me to another soul until you are certain you can trust them.

"I worked for the Society for my entire adult life. My father brought me into it when I turned eighteen, although he'd been preparing me for much longer than that. We were warriors, fighting the good fight, or so we thought. The forces of evil were to be beaten back on every side, at any cost, and there were none more evil than those creatures from the Other Side. Hideous, malformed things they are. If you've never seen one, then thank your lucky stars. Glimpses Over There can wreck a man's sanity, even before he can battle them. But it had to be done. These things had to be stopped before they broke through here and cause more chaos and mayhem than they already had. Two World Wars had been enough for mankind, and if these things came through... That'd be a fight humanity itself might lose.

"The terrors and evils of the creatures we fought were many. Their minds are not like ours, and they feel neither pity nor mercy. Little did I realise that I and the very people I fought alongside were becoming the same.

"Oh, we told ourselves it was all for the best, that it was a necessary evil that we did to prevent a far greater one, but it went too far, too fast." His head lowered, tears sparked in his eyes. "Some of us were lost to darkness almost at once, their minds broken and their spirits turned to evil. They were the lucky ones. Those who tried to deny the awfulness of what they did had a slower and more insidious descent in store. I forget when I realised how far I'd fallen. Maybe when I no longer experienced pain or sadness at the loss of a friend? Maybe when I no longer cared for the names of the people we used and cast aside? But one day I realised I was lost. I was barely human, not worthy of the name any longer, and I had to rescue myself. I tried to remember the man I once was, the feelings he had known for his wife, his family, his grandson. It was all gone. I'd kept my mind, but lost my heart, my soul. I had to prevent others being damned as I was.

"I had a certain amount of influence in the Society, and people listened to me. I talked to a few trusted associates about my fears, and they were sympathetic. I urged them to hold on to their humanity, to resist the darker side of what we were doing and try to bring the Society back to what it had always been intended as: a shining light of hope and a force for good. A small group of us gathered together to work out a new manifesto, put together a list of the activities that were destroying those who carried them out, and we presented it to the Council. They had been on the front lines themselves in quieter times, so they appreciated the risks we ran and the perils we faced just as they understood the toll our duty took. They banned certain practices outright, outlawed them as immoral and dangerous, everything we'd hoped. There were complaints, protests from those who argued we needed to use every trick in our arsenal to fight back against the greater evil facing us, but they were few, the last of their generation and set in their ways. Most of our fellows were in agreement and we had saved them from the darkness we saw in our own future.

"We were so very wrong. They continued with everything they'd always done, now behind closed doors. Reports were censored, the experimenters sworn to secrecy and moved away from supervision. The entire time we thought we'd diverted the Society from its dark and doomed path, they were marching back down it faster than ever. When I found out a few years later, when I caught one of the younger men using vivisection on an innocent woman to create a better weapon, I was horrified. I should have been more suspicious, should have looked deeper, but I genuinely believed..." His voice trailed off. He took a deep breath and continued. "Or maybe I didn't want to know.

"I took that horror back to the Council. I insisted on them dropping these practices, but in the course of an angry confrontation I realised that they'd only been keeping me around to use me as much as possible, assuming that either I'd die in service or burn out, or perhaps come over to their way of thinking with just a gentle nudge. The head of the Society, Mr Green, left me in no doubt that my usefulness had ended if I was unwilling to go along with their position. I stormed out, gathered what items and artefacts I could lay my hands on, and left that place forever."

He'd left the Society? Green was involved in horrific, immoral activities? I had no time to think, I couldn't ask for a moment to gather my thoughts.

"I took a few of my closest and most trusted allies with me, just a handful of us against the might of the Society. We were foolish, idealistic and not as young or strong as we used to be, but we hoped we could still somehow save our former colleagues. At first we believed the rot was just a few people. After the deception was revealed we knew it encompassed the Council, but not how wide it truly was. Every attempt we made to recruit was blocked, everyone we approached to sound out about their feelings rebuffed us. We were alone. We had the moral high ground, for what that was worth, and not much else.

"I set up a research centre at my home for us to use, warded against discovery, and sought ways to continue the fight without embracing the darkness. We were making progress too. We'd left one or two people on the inside and they provided specimens and books for us from time to time, and I had been researching for years. Then the attacks started.

"Fae would single us out, even when they had no reason to. Left to their own devices, the Fae are directionless. They'll attack if they feel threatened, and they're nasty, but they'll run off if they think they're outmatched, and they'll never strike a well-armed group in broad daylight. These did. They were being controlled, driven at us by someone who knew us. Our moles inside the Society knew nothing about it, claimed there was no-one inside who was orchestrating attacks. We discovered that some poor souls who had all but lost their minds had escaped from containment, but they didn't pose an organised threat to us. It was quite some time before we learned that one had been released deliberately and sent after us. And this devil was not as harmless as we'd supposed."

Olivia. It had to be. But deliberately released?

"Three of us were dead before we understood what we were facing. Fae attacks more vicious than ever before. They were being driven to destroy us at all costs. It took weeks of searching, all the while in terror of the next attack. By the end we were down to just two, but we found him. We cornered him in Exeter, and he fought us to the end."

He?

"With him gone, the attacks eased off again, but the damage was done. We were no longer even as effective as we'd been before, and the Society wrote us off. But we weren't done yet."

He looked off to one side and nodded to someone unseen.

"I am running out of time, but it was important you learned what I'd done, and why. The Society once did useful work, it's true, but at a terrible cost. You must be careful, they won't trust you if they learn what I've told you. I'm sorry you're involved now, truly I am, but your bloodline makes you more important to this fight than you know.

"I have to go, with luck there'll be time for another message. But remember, trust nobody in the Society, no matter how harmless they may seem. For now, you're on your own unless you can reach the one person I still trust."

He motioned off to the side, his arm invisible below the elbow. Another figure coalesced beside him, a woman his own age. Her striking green eyes were sparkling as she looked towards me.

"This is Olivia Green," my grandfather said. "And I trust her with my life."

Chapter Eighteen

A Desperate Situation

The images faded from sight, and I found myself back in the living room of my house. The card crumbled away and I wiped the dust from my fingers. I couldn't make sense of what I'd just learned. Olivia had been an ally of my grandfather, and not his killer? Or had he misplaced his trust, been fooled by her and ultimately betrayed? And then there was everything he'd said about the Society's true nature and his opposition to it. Green had always implied that Grandad was a loyal member, dedicated to bringing down Olivia.

Tina said something I didn't catch.

Trust nobody, he'd said. "How long was I... out?" I asked.

"Just a moment, your face went blank. That was a vision card, wasn't it? I've never seen one in real life. Who was it from?"

"My grandfather," I croaked. "He must have left it in this book for me to find some day."

Tina smiled. "Thank goodness, I worried it might have been from, you know, her."

As much as I wished to trust her, I needed time to understand what I'd learned. "No, nothing to do with Olivia," I lied. "He explained about his secret life, gave me some information about the Society and a few more personal messages. It's lucky I had run into you lot already.

If that would have been my introduction to the world of magic, I don't know what I would have thought. Enough distractions, let's find my wife."

Mr Green still stood on the lawn outside. A curtain twitched at a neighbour's window, so I invited him and Mr Blue into the house.

"What do we do now?" I asked.

Mr Green spoke first. "We assume that Olivia's protected against being traced. We've had no luck finding her so far."

"Right, but this is a somewhat unique situation," Tina replied, with a nod to me. "She reached out."

"You think she'll contact me again? She must want something from me, to take my wife."

"She was reckless coming out of hiding." It was a surprise to hear Mr Blue speaking with such a high-pitched voice for his stocky build.

Green nodded agreement. "Maybe she thinks you are an easy target, unable to fight back, which would make her careless."

"What can I do?" I asked. "If I'm an easy target then train me, get me ready to face her!"

"You've done enough," Green snapped. "Doing any more magic will only expose you to her further. Not to mention that if you're our only link to her, we can't afford to risk you. In fact, I insist that you stay at the Society's offices from now on. It's not safe here, and I won't put any more of my men in danger guarding you."

"I'll stay here with him," Tina said. "I'm not one of 'your men'."

Green turned to face her. "And continue your unofficial lessons in an even more unprotected location? Absolutely not."

I hadn't expected that he'd agree to teaching me, but keeping me confined was unexpected. Then again, if we were all together at the

Society, it might make it easier to decide who to trust. And I could look into what my grandfather had told me and determine the truth of the situation. "I'll come back to the office," I said. "Just let me pack a bag, and we can go."

Tina followed me up the stairs and, when she judged we were out of earshot, grabbed my arm.

"What, now you don't trust me?" she asked. "After I put my job on the line to help you out, you go running back to Green for his protection?"

"No, it's not like that," I protested, praying my face didn't betray the lie. "I just don't want you taking any more risks on my behalf."

We gathered in my office where Marlin had brought us tea, now stone cold in the cups. Tina voted for a full assault, taking the fight to Olivia head-on. Green's primary concern was getting my wife to safety rather than fighting Olivia, and he considered a frontal attack too risky. Blue agreed and suggested an infiltration of her hiding place and a rescue of the 'hostage'. I wondered about his former life for a moment before I realised Green was asking my opinion.

"Until we can find her, it's all moot. We can't make a plan until we know what we're facing, can we? What if she contacts me again? Can't we trace the call or something?"

"There are ways to narrow down a location, but they're not precise," Green said, "and we'd need to monitor you closely. In the meantime I suggest you keep busy, get on with your usual work and leave everything to us."

The last thing I wanted to do was carry on as normal, but I didn't argue. It gave me a chance to investigate. One advantage of my computerised system was that it let me hunt through reports and memos that I'd digitised for patterns in the actions of the Society. A few carefully worded searches turned up nothing. Until now I'd been concentrating on newer reports, figuring they would be more useful than historical records, but those were the ones my grandfather had suggested were most likely to have been censored.

Now I requested a cross-section of reports from various decades to give me a good view of whether anything unsavoury had been going on in the past. I hoped that this would be innocuous enough to avoid any suspicion. Marlin couldn't see over the stack of boxes on his wheeled trolley when he delivered them that afternoon.

"Thanks for these. Hey, seen any good movies lately?" I asked him.

"*The Shop Around The Corner*," he replied. "It's much better than *You've Got Mail*."

"Yeah, but Meg Ryan's always great," I countered. "*Sleepless in Seattle*? A classic!"

"No, give me Margaret Sullivan every time. Better chemistry with Jimmy Stewart than Ryan ever did with Tom Hanks."

The top box dated from the 1950s and even scanning the first few of the reports within turned my stomach inside out. The first I checked mentioned 'Sedgwick's Method' to seal a weak point by a standing stone in Wiltshire. It explained that Sedgwick was a magician from the 1880s who had devised a spell to close a portal between Here and There through blood magic. It started with 'the entire contents of a man's veins, daubed around the perimeter of the doorway'. Another turned up a spell which required a 'volunteer as a conduit for the magical energies'. Although, reading further, if the casting of the spell did not kill the 'conduit' outright, they would be left catatonic or insane and I had no doubt that any volunteer would have been anything but.

Page after page turned up similar horrors. Every field report from the 50s required something unspeakable. They sacrificed people, desecrated bodies, magically forced people to perform horrific acts upon each other to lure creatures to the carnage. Even children were not safe. In horror I checked the later decades, hoping that I might find that this one box had been an aberration, that later reports might show that I'd chanced across a particularly awful period. The reports from the 60s were just as bad, the 70s even worse, and even the 1980s were nauseating to read. Only in the 1990s did more innocuous practices and references to substitute magical components appear. This was around the time when my grandfather attempted to put a stop to things, and either stopped such practices, or only driven them underground. Green would know which, but I couldn't trust him. Tina I wanted to believe was trustworthy, but as an outsider with as little information as I did couldn't help me. My mind spinning, I elected to see whether there was any news yet.

"Nothing," Green told me when I tracked him down. "She just wants you to stew for a while, so get some rest if you can while we keep watch."

I'd never known the Society had rooms available for their members to sleep in, but the sparsely furnished room looked welcoming enough, if small. This part of the offices overlooked Battersea Power Station, thick black smoke issuing from the chimneys showing this was a view from many years ago.

The tattered armchair lurched under me, so I took my chances on the bed. The mattress was soft and yielding, the springs creaking as I sat. I was certain I wouldn't sleep.

A knock on the door woke me.

I was still dressed, my legs dangling over the end of the bed. With a grunt, I hauled my aching limbs over to the door and opened it. Tina stood there with two steaming mugs.

"Morning sleepyhead," she smiled. "Now, don't get angry."

"Why would I be angry? You've brought coffee."

"I thought you needed some sleep, and I figured you wouldn't be able to relax, so I... well, I..." she tailed off.

"You cast a spell to put me to sleep," I said.

"I didn't want to, but Green..."

"It's OK," I said, taking a sip of the coffee. It wasn't, but I would have been no use to Claire if I hadn't slept. "You didn't have much choice after the trouble I've got you into. Is there any news?"

"Nothing, sorry." She waited, shifting from foot to foot.

"What is it?" I asked.

"I wanted to ask what happened," Tina said. "Not at the house, I mean with you and... her."

I sighed. "How long have you got? The quick version is she doesn't feel she can trust me. I made a poor decision, and it ripped us apart." I blinked back tears, and Tina didn't probe any further.

When I returned to my research, Marlin had delivered another teetering pile of boxes for me. I didn't need to go past the first one as a yellowed piece of paper sat on top of the files within.

Memorandum to all field personnel — CONFIDENTIAL
As you recall, there are those amongst the higher echelons of the Society who find some of our tried-and-trusted methods 'distasteful' and 'unseemly'. As such, they have decided that the following activities are to be outlawed, effective immediately, and replaced with more 'acceptable' practices.

- *Use of human bodies/parts thereof*

- *In particular use of vagrants/undesirables for provision of same*

- *Coercion or tricking/glamouring of bystanders*

- *Blood magic with repercussions on any other than the caster*

- *Interaction or communication with any creature or individual from Over There*

From this date it is required to discontinue these and materially similar methods.
Memorandum to all field personnel — CONFIDENTIAL

This could have been reassuring evidence that the Society had changed their methods, were it not for the hand-written note underneath:

These edicts can be ignored if you feel necessary, under strict secrecy. No reference to be made in reports.

Everything my grandfather had told me was true.

Chapter Nineteen

A Dangerous Plan

This memo should not have been in the box, which meant someone was sneaking me the information I needed. My grandfather had mentioned moles inside the Society, but I'd assumed Green had purged them. If one or more were still here, might I reach out to them somehow? They'd used my document requests to get to me, but left me no means to contact them.

An idea struck me. We were waiting for Olivia to call me, but that's not what happened last time. I'd given her a channel to reach me, and she'd taken it. That should work again, shouldn't it? But I couldn't just go it alone. Even though I couldn't trust him, I needed Green's approval. Another unofficial use of magic on my part would definitely not be ignored, and I'd need him to trace Olivia if took the bait.

I collected Tina on my way. It wasn't clear whether I could trust her either, but my instincts told me I should. And besides, I'd need her help.

Green proved as reluctant as I'd feared. "Let me get this straight. You want to repeat your last remote viewing spell, open a path to our greatest enemy and let her view the inside of our offices?" he asked.

"She's seen it all before, she used to work here," I said. "And besides, what's she going to learn from watching me? That I'm not very good at magic and want my wife back?"

Tina stepped forward. "No-one's been able to track her down yet. Richard's the only one of us she's ever reached out to, and this will give us a chance to trace her location. If he does it inside here, with all of our resources we should be able to find her."

Green buried his face in his hands. "And if she attacks? What then?"

"She won't," I said with confidence. "She wants to talk to me, I'm sure of it."

"And we're only using a viewing spell," Tina added. "The worst she can do is show him something unpleasant." I swallowed hard at the possibility of what she might show me.

"Very well," Green said after a lengthy pause. "Keep her talking as long as you can, so our traces can locate her. And do it in the Divide. That way she can't see anything which might help her."

Thanking him, I pulled Tina out of the room and along the corridor. In the centre of the white room, I readied myself to cast the seeing spell. It took me an age to calm myself enough to feel the surge of energy building. I wasn't trying to peer inside a box this time, I was trying to find Claire. Tina and I agreed that leaving the spell undirected would make it easier for Olivia to intercept it. It also had the benefit of being something I was likely to try, which might fool Olivia into not realising the Society was behind it.

A confusing jumble of images, sounds and smells overwhelmed me, as the spell reached beyond the walls of the building. People scurried across a footbridge in London, and I heard the songs of the buskers and calls of the beggars who lined the bridge. I passed a cafe and smelt the fresh coffee grounds. As I pushed the range of the spell still further, the impressions came faster, each one harder to cling on to, and my focus slipped. Remembering the advice Tina had given me, I tried to relax and let the sensations wash over me. While I was unlikely to find Claire, the further I pushed, the more likely I was to catch Olivia's attention.

The longer I tried, the simpler it was to direct my attention, pushing this way and that to sweep across the country in waves. Just when I seemed to be getting the hang of it, everything disappeared, only a bright white glow in the distance remaining. Olivia walked out of the light and appraised me, judging whether I was worth bothering with. I hoped Green's traces and tripwires were setting off magical alarms in the office right now.

"Where's my wife?" I asked. She continued her inspection without a word. "If you've hurt her, I swear I'll…"

"You couldn't do a thing to me, young man. But your wife is fine. She's sleeping. It's so much easier that way. No awkward questions like who are you, what you think you're doing, are you a witch and so forth." She chuckled to herself.

I gritted my teeth. "What do you want?"

"To talk, nothing more."

"I have nothing to say to you!"

"Ah, but I have a great deal to say to you, Richard. And I couldn't say very much on the train. I said not to dig too deep, didn't I?"

"That was you? But… they told me you killed him!"

"I suppose I did. Your grandfather trusted me with his life, but I failed him when he needed me the most. I never considered they'd go after him. They were happy to pursue me, they thought me mad and dangerous, but him? I always assumed they'd want him back. Little did I realise that they'd stop at nothing to prevent me from using him.

"Your grandfather was one of the most powerful magicians I've ever known, after myself. The idea of his abilities being turned against them was too much for the stuffy old boys to allow. So they eliminated him. Someone inside the Society may have made the attack, but I wouldn't blame you if you hated me for his death. I know I do."

I hoped that the traces didn't extend as far as allowing Green to overhear us. "How can I believe anything you tell me? If you claim to be on my side, why did you take my wife?"

"That was an accident. I just went to drop off that vision card, I didn't realise she'd be there. But it worked to get your attention," she replied.

"Let her go!" I shouted. "You've had your chat, let her go."

"I will. But I'm not finished with you yet. We still have to stop my husband and his cronies. I assume by now you believe what they're up to?"

It was important to assume they'd be monitoring whatever I said. I spoke carefully. "I've seen reports, about how they're working to stop the Fae threat."

"Oh, you've scarcely scratched the surface, dear boy. But I'd better go before your friends complete their trace. I'll be in touch again soon."

With that, she was gone. My spell collapsed around me, and I was back in the marble room again. I brushed aside Tina's questions and primed the Divide to take me home. She protested that I needed to speak to Green, that they might have a location for Olivia, but my only concern was checking on my wife.

"I'm leaving, you can either come with me or explain to Green why you let me go."

I had to spend the entire journey from the exit to my home answering Tina's endless questions. She wanted me to share everything I'd seen and heard. Why Olivia had released my wife extracting no promises or information in return? And she worried that I'd let something slip that might harm us. Then she wanted to know how Olivia had looked. Did she look tired, as if she had been doing a lot of magic? Was she angry, confused, manic? I begged her to stop, just for a moment, while I took comfort in my wife's release and she apologised, embarrassed.

When I got home, Claire was not as pleased to see me as I was to see her. While I'd spent the last day or more worried sick about her, I had no idea what she thought had been happening. My clumsy attempts to find out, or make sure she wasn't hurt or traumatised by her experience just angered her.

"But are you OK?" I asked. "I mean, after that fright last night…"

She rolled her eyes at me. "I'm fine, it was just the fog, like you said. Why are you suddenly concerned?"

"I still care about you, you know."

"You were quick enough to dash off to work without a backwards glance. And now you bring someone new home with you," she pointed at Tina, who had been trying to make herself invisible, "to check up on me, you claim? Just leave me alone, will you?" She pulled her front door key from her keyring and flung it at me before walking to the front door. As she stepped through, she looked back over her shoulder at me. "And if you're happy enough to move on, you can sign the damn papers!" The door slammed behind her.

"She's fine, then?" Tina asked after a moment.

"Good as ever," I muttered. "Let's go back and talk to Green."

It took over an hour to tell Tina and Mr Green everything I was comfortable sharing. I didn't see any harm in telling them that Olivia planned to bring down the Society, or that she denied killing my grandfather. I stopped short of telling them she'd all but blamed Green for that. I let them know that she'd suggested she'd contact me again, and that tracing her would be futile.

"Did you get a location?" I asked.

Green sighed. "We did, but even though we sent a team there straight away, there was no sign of her. Either she misdirected us, which is supposed to be impossible, or she cleared out immediately."

"What now?"

"We're sending in two of our best researchers. Think of them like a forensic team. They'll see if there's any trace we can use, and I'd like you to go with them. It should be safe, but frankly if you're there, and she really wants to communicate, then it might bring her out of hiding again. Be on your guard."

Chapter Twenty

A Revealing Excursion

By the time I reached reception Mr Green was already there. He was deep in conversation with another elderly man in a very sharp three-piece suit, black raincoat and patent leather shoes, who he introduced as Mr Red. Green didn't exhibit his usual confidence, looking up at the taller man like a child seeking approval. Red took my hand, his cheerful mood evaporating. Evidently not everyone shared Mr Green's enthusiasm for letting me tag along. As I contemplated how to win him over, a flustered old woman hurried along the corridor behind us, apologising for keeping us waiting.

Introduced as Mrs Orange, she had the air of an absent-minded Grandmother about her. I half expected to see knitting needles poking out of her handbag and was sure there were toffees in there somewhere.

"So you're Howard's grandson," Orange said. "I'm sorry for your loss. He was a talented man, I liked him."

"He was a capable researcher. Right, we have a lot to do today. Keep up," Red barked, and strode away. I looked over at Mrs Orange, and she patted my arm encouragingly before scurrying off after him. Saying goodbye and thanks to Mr Green, I followed my new colleagues into the Divide and asked where we were going.

"Harrogate." With that Red lit the powder which he'd mixed with a crumbling piece of cake, opened the door in front of us, before picking up a doctor's bag and stepping through. Orange and I stepped out into blinding sunshine. When my eyes adjusted, I saw we were stepping from a bin storage area behind Betty's Tea Shop. Mrs Orange smiled, and said to me, "I like their fruitcake, you know, and it brings us right to the centre of town."

We had to walk a fair distance to our destination. I removed my jacket in the warm sun, but Mr Red kept on his long black raincoat. On the way, Mrs Orange brought me up to speed with Olivia's recent activities. She'd been busy. The number of attacks by other-worldly creatures had intensified, and this was stretching the Society too thin to deal with the recent incidents. As a result, Orange informed me, stories and rumours were circulating in the civilian population and it was only a matter of time before someone noticed something that the Society couldn't explain away.

"Are things that bad?"

"Yes, they are, although we're not meant to discuss it," Mr Red said with a scowl at Mrs Orange. She frowned back, then grinned at Red's obvious discomfort.

"He was bound to find out, it's not exactly a secret. Mr Green's just worried about spooking the new lad," she explained to me. "But you can handle it, can't you dear?" she said, patting my arm again.

"Of course!" I said.

Mr Red scoffed. He marched on in silence, but Mrs Orange more than compensated by telling me about her grandchildren, one of whom had just given her a great-grandchild. I wasn't able to keep track of which names were her offspring, which their partners, who was with whom but shouldn't have been, and who wasn't treating who correctly and was, in her words, 'a bad one'. It was a pleasure to hear someone talking with such enthusiasm though, and I was glad of the distraction.

The purported hideout was a disused warehouse at the end of a potholed road near the edge of town, with warning signs marking it as unsafe to enter. The walls were peeling paint, layer upon layer revealing the history of the place in changing colours. A few safety notices were legible through years of grime and mould, extorting the workers to 'Avoid Slips and Trips' and 'Be Aware'. A rusted corrugated iron roof let in shafts of sunlight in which flies and motes of dust danced, and also let in the rain as puddles of grimy water pooled across the stained concrete floor. The entire place smelled like a toilet to me, and I suspected that was the primary use of this building now. Why would someone stay here if they had the means to travel anywhere they wanted?

"Don't touch anything," Red barked. He set to work with some magic I couldn't follow, pausing only to reprimand me for missteps real and imagined. After a while he made a sound which suggested he'd found something interesting that he wanted me to ask about. Despite my curiosity, I refused and treasured my insignificant victory when he broke his silence.

"She was here, but some time ago. She's covered her tracks too well for us to follow, so this entire trip has been a waste of time." He bagged up a few minor items, old till receipts or printed notes, and then announced we should get back. He strode over to the foreman's office in the warehouse's corner and with a muttered incantation pulled open the door to show the familiar corridor back through the Divide. Mrs Orange and he stepped through, and with a last look around I followed.

Instead of the bright light of the Divide, I came to a thin plywood door coated in nicotine-stained white paint. There was no handle, no lock. I pushed it open to reveal a rundown room in a tumbledown warehouse, just like the one I had left. A battered wooden desk sat opposite me, a folding chair in front of it. The roof of the small office dripped into puddles around the desk, and the walls were swollen with damp and riddled with green mould. The entire room stank of decay and rot.

Olivia sat behind the desk. "Hello Richard, I apologise for the hijacking," she chuckled. "But I don't want to keep chatting when we might be overheard, and your associates are far too keen to get their hands on me."

"How did you...?" I pulled my phone from my pocket, but with a wave of her hand it flew across the room and smashed against a rusted filing cabinet.

"Now, now," she purred. "I can hardly have you calling your friends, can I? We're going to have a pleasant chat. Tea?" I looked at the chipped teapot and stained mugs on the desk and declined. "Straight to it, good man. I want you to work with me to bring down the Society, just like your grandfather."

"You don't want much then," I replied. "Just betray the people who've been keeping me safe from you this whole time, is that it?"

"They've been doing a grand job, don't you think?"

"You're the one who's killing them!"

She waved a hand dismissively. "They didn't leave me any choice. They wouldn't let me in to your house without fighting, so I turned them inside out. It was quick," she added, "they wouldn't have felt it for long."

"You kidnap my wife, hijack me, kill God knows how many people and expect me to come and join you? You really are insane, aren't you?"

Anger flashed in her green eyes. "No! I'm the only one who's sane, the only one who sees reality as it is. The only one who knows the horror that awaits us if those, those... idiots get their way!"

I scoffed.

"You still don't know what they're doing, do you? Goodness me, I tried to spell it out to you. Who do you think hid those reports so you wouldn't see the things they did? All the experiments, stealing bodies from graveyards, morgues, and even people off the streets. They would not let you know about all that, Richard."

"That still doesn't justify what you're doing. They have to stop those... things from Over There getting through, and you're opening the door to them!"

She shook her head. "Richard, Richard, the Society are the real monsters. They want power. They had it before and they want it again. Back in the dark ages their kind were all-powerful conquerors, King-makers, Empire-crushers. With the spells at their disposal, they ruled whole continents. Not in the open, of course, not when people had a habit of stringing up or burning someone just for trying to cure a wart. No, as the power behind the throne. It suited the people much better to think Napoleon was a great General, or that God chose Charlemagne to rule rather than believe in some shadowy cabal.

"But they couldn't survive. Technology, science, engineering distracted those who would have been called to magic in earlier ages. Their numbers dwindled, and they lost knowledge. A few carried on in secret, but as superstition declined, so too did those willing to entertain the idea of another world beyond our own. They formed societies like the one you're so quick to defend, pretended to be eccentric clubs for the wealthy to avoid any suspicion, but they lost their grip on the reins of power. Mr Green wants that power back."

"Even if that's true, he won't tell me all about it. He doesn't trust me any more than I trust him."

"Which is why you need to be convincing when you go to my dear sweet psychopath of an ex-husband and beg him to let you kill me. I need him to believe. He knows whose blood runs in your veins, and you are their best bet to stop me. If you had sufficient motive to want me destroyed, he'd show you everything in his arsenal to enable you to do it. So that's what I will give you. Motive." She stepped back and raised both hands, her eyes filling with black as she grinned at me. "This may hurt a bit."

Chapter Twenty-One

A Painful Approach

Bolts of light shot from her fingertips and engulfed me. Every single nerve ending screamed in agony, pain overwhelming my mind. I fell to the floor, tried to roll away, beat out the flames engulfing me. I tried to summon up energy to build a defence, but she just stripped it away from me and intensified her assault. Time slowed to a crawl, I don't know how long I lay there screaming before she stopped. My entire skin burned, and I wanted to die.

"That should do the trick," she said, and knelt beside me. She whispered, "They should believe you want me dead now, don't you think? And they'll trust you at last. Off you go, dear."

I don't remember the trip back through the Divide. Only a vague jumble of images and sensations filtered through the agony. I had a hazy recollection of stumbling along the corridor, screaming each time my abused flesh touched the walls. Eventually the white-tiled room materialised around me. And then, nothing.

I awoke in the bed in my temporary room, Tina and Mr Green looking

down at me with worried expressions, while Mrs Orange was ban-
daging my legs. She had swathed my body in bandages glowing with
magical energy, ugly scarred flesh visible between. I wanted to touch
my aching face, but something wrapped my hands like mittens.

I tried to speak, but only a croak emerged. Tina looked away, her
eyes full of tears. Green was more stoic. "You were lucky," he said, "we
reconstructed your face, and your other burns will heal in time too.
I guess she didn't want you dead." I mimed a bubble around myself,
put my hands up as if blocking a punch, and gave Tina a thumbs up.
Even that short effort exhausted me.

"I'm glad my lessons let you defend yourself," Tina sniffed and
dabbed her eyes. "I just wish..." Her voice broke. I nodded, and my
head swam. Evidently I was on powerful painkillers.

"Don't let her reaction worry you," Green reassured me, "it's not
as bad as all that. You'll be able to speak again in a few hours when
the healing spells on your face do their work and you should be up
and about again within a day or so. There will be some scars, but you
were fortunate it wasn't worse. I hate to admit it, but Ms Black might
have been right to prepare you after all. I believed Olivia would ignore
you if she didn't see you as a threat, so I didn't want to make you one.
That ship has sailed though." He turned and walked towards the door,
pausing with his hand on the doorknob. "Get some rest and we'll talk
more when you feel better."

As the bandages covered the last patches of burnt skin, a cooling
wave soothed my entire body. Mrs Orange muttered something I
didn't catch, and I slipped into a deep and dreamless sleep.

As Green had promised, within two days I could get out of bed again. My face had healed and most of my body was free from scars, although a few white marks across my back remained. My left leg however was still twisted and painful, requiring me to use a stick to move around. Mrs Orange explained her healing abilities only stretched so far, but I was grateful she had managed the miracles she had.

I was keen to get back to my studies, but I decided that this time I would not try to study in secret. It would be best to ask Green for formal permission to continue. Not only would that put my training on a more official footing, but it would also enable me to test whether my injuries had convinced him to trust me. If Olivia was right, the Society would be keen to make the most of my abilities to their own ends. All I had to do was convince Green, and I decided to enlist Tina to help me. Fortunately she agreed with my idea, and soon we stood side by side in Green's office, like two school kids in front of the headmaster.

I spoke first. "Unless I was hallucinating at the time, I remember you saying Ms Black had been right to teach me magic. Her defensive spells were all that saved me from Olivia's attack. Since Olivia clearly views me as a threat to her plans now, I want to learn more."

"He needs to learn offensive spells too," Tina said. "It's all well and good being able to defend himself but he has to be able to strike back."

"You two have given this a lot of consideration, I take it?" Green smiled. "As it happens, I agree." Tina and I exchanged a grin.

"Thank you," I said. "The more I learn the better, now I've had a taste of what we're up against."

"Yes," said Green. "And if you hadn't come in to see me already, I was going to ask you if you were willing to step up your training a notch. We should discuss what it is you learn, and for that matter, where."

"Excuse me?" Tina asked.

"If I'm going to join this fight, I want to do it properly." I said.

Green nodded. "You need to learn fast, I think we all agree on that, and while Ms Black may be an adequate tutor, her skills can only take you so far." Tina gasped, and I risked a peek at her. Her jaw was clenched tight and her eyes bored into Green. "Meet me at the Divide in five minutes."

Thanking him, I left the office and braced for the explosion. Tina rounded on me as soon as the door was closed.

"What the hell?" she yelled. "Was that your plan all along? Get me to back you up then kick me out?"

"No! I honestly assumed I'd just come back and work with you again, I did not expect he would suggest someone else." I wished I could explain how this was for the best, that I needed to dig deeper to find out the truth and that this could prove to be my best opportunity.

"After I put my damn job on the line for you, skulked around in secret for you to teach you how to defend yourself, which saved your bloody life by the way, you're welcome. You know how they treat me here, and now you're doing the same?"

"It's not like that," I insisted, "but I need to..."

"Screw you," she shouted over her shoulder, already half-way along the corridor.

"That went well," said Blue's high-pitched voice behind me.

I sighed. "She has a point."

"I gather you're joining the team in Liverpool," Blue said. "Good to have you aboard."

My excitement at visiting another Society location faded when Green, Blue and I passed through the Divide into a reception area identical to the one we'd just left. The plants looked sicker, and a surly man staffed the desk instead of the cheerful Janice. But otherwise I'd have been sure we'd just come around in a circle. Mr Green led off along the hallway with a nod to the man on reception and I scurried after him, my cane skittering as I fought to keep up. There were fewer doors here, further apart. The walls had a more utilitarian appearance than our office. It wasn't even as well-cared for as the headquarters building. We soon reached a sturdy iron door which filled the end of the passageway. Mr Blue moved his hands over it in an intricate pattern I couldn't follow, and a loud click indicated it had opened. He stepped aside to allow Green to lead us through.

This was more like it! We stood on a gridded metal walkway above a large open space, dotted with benches and various bits of equipment both magical and scientific. People in lab coats scurried around, or stood absorbed in various experiments they were observing. Cells covered two of the outside walls, each with a large transparent door in front. Given the size of the creatures inside, I hoped it was something stronger than glass. The wall ahead of us had further steel doors set into it, blocking the view of whatever lay beyond. Either more corridors, more rooms, or labs perhaps. Or where they kept the things that needed stronger cages.

It was exactly what I'd imagine if I pictured a secret magical research base and it filled me with glee. Mr Green coughed to get my attention before gesturing to one side, and we descended a spiral staircase.

My eyes kept flitting around the room, until something caught my attention and stopped me in my tracks. I paused with my left foot half-way between two steps, my cane already on the next stair down, and clutched at the handrail for support. At the base of the stairs was a figure who towered over those around him, wider than a doorway across the shoulders, wearing an oversized white lab coat which strained at the seams. As he dealt with various enquiries, I noted his skin and hair so pale as to be pure white, and a single row of horns running in a decreasing series from his head and along his neck. A row of gentle bumps in the back of his lab coat suggested they continued the full length of his spine. My leg wobbled under me, and I descended the last few steps in a rather ungraceful manner.

"You thought Marlin was the only Fae we employed?" Green laughed. "They do more than just make tea, you know. Come on, let me introduce you. Byron, come and meet a fresh recruit."

The figure turned and crossed the distance between us in a few lengthy strides. Close up, he looked even more demonic. He wore no shoes on his hoofed feet, and his hands bore fingers twice as long as I'd expect them to be, and more of them than was usual. "It is a pleasure to meet you," he boomed out. His voice was deep, I felt it reverberate in my chest as much as I heard it in my ears. He thrust out his hand, and I reached to shake it. His grip was gentle, although the sensation of his long supple fingers wrapping all the way around my hand and over my wrist was very peculiar. As he released his grip, I saw small round suckers like an octopus, ranging in size from almost invisible to the size of my thumbnail covering his fingers. I suppressed a shudder.

"Byron is one of our best researchers," Green said. "He is always telling me he needs more help, and so I thought of you." He turned to face Byron again and continued "Mr Brown here comes from a worthy lineage, and he has talent."

"I have heard," Byron said. "To survive an attack from our Adversary takes a certain level of ability." He spoke distinctly, with no trace of an accent. Did Fae have accents?

"We figured he would do well to follow you around for a while, learn the ropes," Green was saying. "Perhaps you will show him around the place and let him see what you get up to. I have to be getting back," he added with a glance at his pocket watch. "Have fun!"

Byron regarded me carefully, in the manner of a dog sizing up a bone. I shifted awkwardly under his gaze. "Shall we begin?" he asked, leading me over to a vast metal door beneath the staircase. He pushed the door open. We stepped through and I stifled a scream.

Chapter Twenty-Two

A Gruesome Revelation

My injured leg wobbled under me as my head spun. Reading the old reports of the Society's worst excesses hadn't prepared me for this, no matter what I'd thought. There were creatures of all shapes and sizes strapped to angled metal surfaces. Some had tubes running into their limbs, like IV drips in a hospital patient, though I doubted the substances being pumped in were for their benefit. Others had thicker tubes protruding from their bodies, which dripped and oozed foul-looking substances into waiting bags. None of the beings in the room appeared awake, but they moaned in pain. Injuries abounded. Some were bruised, while others had cuts both deep and shallow covering their bodies. Nobody had made any attempt to clean or dress their wounds, and more than a few showed signs of infection and disease. These were Byron's kin. Did he feel nothing?

"Here is where we get most of our more exotic supplies," he explained, his deep voice untroubled. "Some of these creatures secrete valuable substances of which we can make use, so we keep them here to harvest what we need. They don't last long, but they are plentiful enough to ensure we never run out."

"You don't keep them alive?" I asked. "Farmers don't kill their cows or chickens, after all… Oh, until they stop producing."

"Exactly. Since we are taking their vital essences, they cannot survive long. One of our challenges is working out better yields from each specimen, or which species gives the most before it dies. To that end we are experimenting with our own breeding program, but there are some who would rather not... enhance the population even under controls like this. They consider it is better to increase the number we capture."

"These certainly seem harmless," I said, trying to keep the disgust from my voice.

"They are now." Byron chuckled. "We keep them pretty well subdued, so long as it does not taint the product. For any which we cannot drug or tie down, we render them safe by other means." He gestured to the back of the room, and my stomach churned. Across the rear of the place were unrestrained creatures. Without their limbs they had no means to move or struggle. The blood clotted on the stumps that remained was black and sticky, and the loudest of the moans came from these beings. I took a deep breath and looked closer, fighting my urge to flee and instead stepping towards them as if to show interest. Someone had sewn their mouths shut with thick twine, jabbed through whatever passed for lips. I wondered if they did that before they amputated the limbs, to save themselves from hearing the screams.

Byron joined me beside one of them, little more than a torso and head. It thrashed about, its stumps smearing viscous black blood on the metal beneath. Tubes ran from several points on the chest and stomach, extracting a dull green liquid, which oozed into a collecting jar. I saw genuine fear in its eyes. Startled to see a human emotion from it, I had to glance away and stared at the green goo in the jar to collect my thoughts.

"That is a very useful material," Byron said, noting my gaze. "When you dry it and crush it into a fine powder, it is one of the primary constituents of the Divide priming gear." I felt sick. Every time I'd used the Divide, I'd been using the fruits of this torture? "These animals are adept at opening portals through from Over There, so your predecessors adapted that ability to form the Divide over a hundred years ago. Almost everything your people learned about magic came from studying creatures like these."

"And what did they learn from you?" I asked, unable to stop myself. "While you were a prisoner here, did they drain you dry too? I see you still have your limbs, at least!"

Byron didn't look surprised. "They realised that I was intelligent, unlike these... beasts, and so they wished to speak with me. Once they resolved the language problems, I could communicate freely, and we came to an arrangement. I am a scientist, after all, and I wished to continue my work. There are those Over There doing the same as you, you must realise. Once we became aware of your existence we studied you, endeavoured to determine what you were and what use you might be. I have spent most of my life in rooms like this, on one side or the other."

Steadying myself on the table, I realised I'd placed my hand into the clotting blood. I had to turn and leave the room before I vomited. "It can be a lot to take in," Byron called from behind me, "so take some fresh air and I will meet you shortly. I have some details to arrange here." I barely heard him as I stumbled to the metal door.

My legs shook under me, and I climbed into the seat behind Byron's desk. It dwarfed me, and my legs dangled inches from the floor. I'd wanted to find out the truth, penetrate the Society's secrets. Be careful what you wish for, I thought. I took huge gulps of air to bring my nausea under control. The ringing in my ears took longer to stop.

Byron opened the steel door and stepped through, smiling at the sight of me in his gigantic chair. "That was too much for you, I think," he boomed. "It is normal, you humans are very sentimental."

"It was a shock," I admitted. "I didn't know what you were doing. Mr Green never said."

"Ah yes, he does love his secrets. But here, you will see everything, and we shall work together on improving your abilities. I can show you how to use your powers and you can show me how you handle magic. We will make an excellent team, you and I. Come."

Byron led me out of his office towards one side of the open space and two of the glass-fronted cells I'd glimpsed from above. One was empty, the other contained a beast like the one I'd seen on my first day. I dredged my memory for the name. "Is that a Chivato?" I asked.

I'd impressed Byron. "It is, although this is a new breed that has been showing up of late in Scotland. We wish to understand how they can evolve so quickly. It takes generations for a species to remodel itself in nature, but these are changing visibly from their parents."

"We breed dogs for different traits, it's possible someone's doing the same for these things." The thought chilled me. The one in the cage looked even meaner than the one I'd met before.

"That was our thought too," Byron replied. "And it is not a pleasant one. If someone were to be producing an army made-to-measure, then we will have to face them one day. That informs the other part of our research, which is how to stop them."

Byron handed over a few folders of notes to a human assistant and spoke with her for a few minutes while I looked around again. I'd need to be patient to uncover the secrets of this place.

"You didn't ask, by the way. Most people do."

"Hmm?" I replied.

"Where I got my name."

"Oh, I just assumed you were a writer of poetry. Or a wild, debauched party lover," I said.

He threw his head back and guffawed, causing the entire room to turn and look, then slapped me on the back. Only my cane enabled me to stay upright.

He apologised. "I do not know my strength. Actually I do, but I often forget human weakness." I told him not to worry and wondered if he'd cracked my shoulder blade.

"So you're not a poet?" I asked. We set off towards the rear of the space and the vast metal doors. It took a while as people asking for Byron's opinion or advice interrupted us.

"It was a nickname coined when I was first captured. They decided I was insane, you see, since they could not understand me, nor I them. And since I am a vicious fighter when cornered, someone described me as 'mad, bad and dangerous'. A pretty poor joke, but from there we got to 'Byron'. Your tongues could not handle my true name, not that I would trust someone with that knowledge."

"But you speak English now."

"One researcher here had an idea for a translation spell. He believed that if he cast it on himself it would render him fluent in any language under the sun, including some mankind had never heard."

"And he cast it on you too?"

"No, it was an abject failure. While he could indeed comprehend any language, he was unable to control which tongue he himself would use to communicate. One word might be French, the next Hindi, the third a dead Mesopotamian language, and the grammar and syntax were indecipherable. He was no use as a translator."

"So how...?"

Byron fished inside his lab coat and pulled out a brown shrivelled twig on a silver chain. After a moment, I realised with disgust that it was a mummified finger.

"Yes, we found his use in the end, although we are now down to a handful of pieces. No pun intended," he said, tucking the grisly item away again. "I speak in my own language, and you comprehend it in whatever your mother tongue might be. This proves very useful for us but must still be kept secret. If everyone in the UN for example understood a speaker in their own language at once, you can imagine the consternation."

"I think they'd be rather more disturbed by the seven foot tall horned guy, personally, but I see your point," I said.

Byron laughed again, his voice rattling the beakers on a nearby desk. "I like you," he guffawed. "Now, shall we start your training? Or do you need more time to settle your nerves?"

Time to prove myself, earn his trust. "I'm fine, I've seen the threat I'm facing and I need to learn how to deal with it. This is no time to be squeamish."

"Excellent!" he bellowed, and I heard the breaking of glass as someone dropped something in surprise. "I have been told of your power, you could be stronger than your grandfather and will do glorious things. Show me!"

"Here?" I said. "I don't want to break something. I almost wrecked a lab once when I lost concentration."

"Quite right. Let us find somewhere more suitable for someone 'dangerous to know', shall we?"

CHAPTER TWENTY-THREE

A NECESSARY EVIL

One of the side doors opened into a long windowless room, empty apart from sandbags piled up against the far wall. Byron sealed the door behind us with a gesture. "Now we are safe," he said, his voice echoing off the bare walls. With a calming breath I centred myself and gathered the energies I'd not used since my injuries.

I started with my well-practised protective bubble, extending it about six inches from my body. Byron's arm snapped out, and his long fingers slammed into the surface of the shield. I could tell he'd struck, but it was more of a slap than a punch. "Not bad," he muttered, and without warning spun around and launched a forceful back-kick at my stomach. His hoofed foot impacted the bubble at speed, but just in time I concentrated my defence on that spot, strengthening the shield. As a result, his kick didn't injure me, but it still caused me to lose my balance. I stepped backward, and as I put the weight on my damaged leg it buckled beneath me. The pain caused my protection to falter and vanish, much of my power escaping before I could re-absorb it. Byron swayed as it passed over him.

"Impressive," Byron conceded. "Although, had I followed up with a second kick, your heart would be over there by now." He gestured to the sandbags. "You must work on your concentration."

"That was the first time I've had to defend myself like that," I explained. "And you are awfully strong."

"Did you not use that spell to defend against Olivia?" he replied.

"I tried, but it wasn't particularly effective," I gestured toward my leg. "It was all a blur when she got me. I reacted on instinct more than anything, I'm not even sure what I did." This much was true.

"If your first reaction was to put up a shield, then your instincts are good. Let me see how you attack now."

I stood up again. "Don't we need a target?" I asked.

"I can fetch you one of my creatures, if you think it would help."

"No, that's fine," I answered, gathering up my remaining energy and facing the sandbags. I visualised bolts of electricity, trying to put out of my mind how it felt to be on the receiving end. Jagged blue arcs flew from my fingertips and stabbed into the sandbags. One exploded, showering damp sand over a small area, others caught fire and charred before my reserves ran out and Byron extinguished the small fires with a gesture. I sagged, relying on my cane to keep me upright. I'd pushed too hard trying to impress him and wasted too much power.

"You're weak," he said. "I accept you are only recently back on your feet, but you should still be stronger. Who instructed you before me?"

"Tina Black."

He nodded. "She is competent. But what did she show you to boost your energies?"

"I don't... I mean, the first time I made a pill from some powder and my blood, but since then it's just been internal energy I've harnessed."

"That unlocks your potential, it does not augment it. You only rely on your own power?" He sounded impressed.

"She said no one should take power from others. It was dangerous, forbidden, and a sign of madness."

Byron scoffed. "Nonsense! To be certain, humans who lose control will grab energies wherever they can, but that is a symptom of their malady and not a cause. They crave power and they will do whatever they have to do to get more of it. But you can take it if you need it, do not worry."

I wasn't sure about this. "Won't it harm the person I take it from?

"And if it does?" Byron retorted. "If it is a matter of survival, then I say choose yourself. In the midst of battle, you will want to be as strong as possible. Come, let me show you."

Byron led me back to his office, and I sank into a chair, rubbing my aching leg.

"You need not suffer when there is power for the taking right here. Observe." He raised his hands towards the creature inside the nearest cell and then stopped. "You know how to observe a magical casting, I assume?"

"I've looked inside a locked box, and I sought out Olivia when she had my wife. Is that the sort of thing you mean?"

"No," he replied. "If you can view the magical flow around you, it will help you understand what you will be doing yourself in a moment. Watch my actions." He lifted his hands again, the creature scurrying to the back corner of the cell as if it foresaw what was coming.

I summoned up the meagre energy I still had and tried to sense what Byron was doing. I glimpsed a wisp of something like smoke leaving the cell and drifting towards him, so I focused and watched as it surrounded his arms. It writhed, twisting and spiralling around those massive hands before vanishing beneath his skin. Shifting my focus, I saw it passing through the glass front of the of the cage and followed it back to the source. The creature inside writhed in pain, thin wisps of its power emerging from all over its body. They joined into thicker strands and twisted together into ropes of magical energy to be absorbed into Byron's arms.

He stopped and lowered his arms. I re-absorbed the energy I'd been using to watch him, feeling even more drained. I could sleep for a week, but I'd have to do it in this chair as I would never make it to a bed.

"Now you. Can you stand?"

"I don't think so," I muttered. "Let me try from here." I raised my arms as my mentor had done and worked to summon up the energies I would need. My shoulders ached, and my arms sagged.

"No! From him, do not use your own," Byron barked. I tried again, this time imagining a thin streamer of smoke from the beast before me. For a while nothing happened, then I noticed a tickle in my forearms as if an insect were crawling over me. I looked down and saw fine wisps caressing my bare skin. My arms were lighter. It was easier to hold them up now than it had been a moment before. I pictured the smoke thickening, and the sensation of movement over my arms intensified. The creature slumped in pain and exhaustion while my entire body grew stronger, and I sat up straighter in my chair. As the energy flowed into me it became easier to pull in more and more, with no care about the beast I was draining. I needed this, I deserved it, didn't I? Before long, my body buzzed as if I'd grabbed a live wire. I was more alive, stronger than I had been in weeks, and I thought my skin must be glowing. My blood pumped faster. I heard my heart beating stronger. I closed my eyes and turned my face to the sky in ecstasy. "That's enough," Byron said, but I wanted, needed more. I directed the flow to my injured leg and imagined it whole again. I pictured the muscles regrowing, the skin knitting and healing just for a moment before the wonderful flow of power was severed. When I opened my eyes, Byron stood with his hand raised. He had cut me off.

It was gone! That wonderful power, that healing had been ripped from me — a glass of water snatched from a man dying of thirst. First came emptiness, followed by a surge of anger greater than I'd known before. How dare he stop me! Who did he think he was? I narrowed my eyes, glared at the giant before me and gathered my stolen energy, ready to attack. It pulsed inside me, strained to be released, begged to be used, to hurt, to maim, to kill. I had to have more, I needed power to fix my leg. The wounds I'd suffered to make sense of this new and dangerous world must be healed. I needed it, and I would take it. I took aim towards Byron.

"I would advise against it," he breathed. My heart pounded, my breathing was shallow and rapid. Every fibre was ready to knock him down, tear out his energy and feast on it. Once I started to feed, I'd drain him and strengthen myself. I could do it. I *would* do it! I readied the strike.

Crash.

I was weak, drained. Ecstasy was replaced with despair. I couldn't attack Byron, I couldn't defend myself, I'd not even formed a shield without knocking Tina across the room. I couldn't do anything, not even look into a box without being hijacked. I was worthless. I was nothing. Byron could crush me like an insect if he wished and I couldn't stop him, I shouldn't even try. I slumped, my arms weak and listless. My head lolled to one side, I lacked the strength to lift it. I would never raise it again, never stand, never walk, never do anything but sit here and die. That was what I deserved.

"I warned you." The words were distant, muffled. Who was speaking? I didn't care, I just wished they'd leave me alone. "I am sorry, but you were about to make a foolish mistake." Of course I was, I was stupid, worthless, useless and weak. I wasn't worth someone wasting time on.

But then, wonderfully, the life came back into me. Not in a flood as before, but a trickle. Like sipping a fine wine, the energy entered me and lifted me out of my depression. I could lift my head again. Wisps of smoke left Byron's hand and curled around me. Wherever they touched, I grew stronger. I was back to normal, not ecstatic as I had been moments before, but out of melancholy. I shook my head. I was myself again, and that was good.

"What the hell was that?" I gasped.

"A valuable lesson," Byron said. "If you try something like that again it will not end well for you."

Chapter Twenty-Four

A Terrifying Lesson

Byron stopped the flow of power. I craved more but knew that even if I dared to try and steal it, he would not let me.

"If you can not learn to control yourself, then you are no better than any other man, and will get yourself killed one way or another."

That overwhelming power, the sense that anything I wanted was mine... I understood how people became addicted to it. "I'll get it under control," I assured him, and shuddered. "I don't want to go through that again."

"Everyone does that the first time," he said, kindness returning to his voice. "It can be overwhelming, and if you do not have someone to hold you back, it can get very nasty. You needed to learn."

"Is that how people lose it? How they go insane, I mean?"

"It is one step along the path. You could not have hurt me, but you would have done so to someone else. You might perhaps have killed someone you cared about. That is difficult to return from. You experienced some of that grief, I think, when the power waned? Even though you had not acted on your desires?"

I nodded, that feeling of utter despair had been as overwhelming as the sense of invulnerability. "Does that happen to everyone?" I asked.

"The path is unique for each, but the destination is the same. Some cannot handle the knowledge of what they did and their minds fracture to protect them from their misdeeds. Others relish in what they did, take pleasure from it. And still others believe the power is under their control until it consumes them."

"But I don't have to end up that way, do I?"

"No, with help and guidance you can learn a modicum of control. But you are very fragile creatures, and magic is not meant for humans. Your minds are the wrong shape for it. You can never control it as we can. You are children playing with matches. Eventually, you all get burnt. Magic, like flame, can be useful, a tool to improve your life. Or it can kill, it can turn on you, burn and scar and damage you, or it can do all of these things at once. You have the ability, I must admit that. There are those among you that do, but you are still not born to it as we are."

"You need to be Fae to use magic properly, is that it?"

"To use it well, yes," he said. "It does not exist in your world, after all. What magic you draw on comes to you from Over There. The power beyond your world is immense. That is why you could pull so much from that creature. He is drenched in it. It runs through his veins, inhabits every cell, pervades his very being."

"And yours too, I guess?"

He grinned and smacked his chest with the flat of his gigantic hand. "I am strong indeed!" he boomed, laughing. "You are feeding on what little slips through the gaps between worlds, but it is still too much for you."

"And if a human went Over There?" I asked. "Would that give them more power?"

Byron glanced around and lowered his voice. "Until recently it was thought to be impossible. We expected that you would be consumed by energies beyond your control. But one of you made the trip and survived."

"Olivia," I whispered.

"Even she did not survive intact. Exactly what happens to your kind, who drink too deep, happened to her much faster. Her mind was fractured, destroyed. When they found her, she was raving mad... but she had brought power back with her. It remains to be seen how much of it she has retained. If you were able to defend yourself against her, then maybe she is weaker again!"

"Yeah, let's hope so!" She had been holding back when she attacked me, but for all I knew she still had as much power as Byron.

"We shall continue another time," he said, "I have things to do now. And you need to rest, no matter how much power I returned to you. We will continue your training tomorrow."

I was halfway up the stairs before I realised I'd left my cane behind.

My sessions with Byron continued as they had begun, with a combination of magical training and practice. Using so much magic put such a strain on me that, despite replenishing my power from the surrounding Fae, my leg always throbbed by the end of the day. I still needed my cane to move around.

Over time, Byron became more forthcoming about what happened in the labs, and one day he even showed me a couple more of the back-rooms.

"None of these things seem dangerous," I said. "But I'm always hearing about attacks and deaths from Fae. Do you not study the nasty ones too?"

"We do, but not here. These laboratories are not equipped for such dangers. We do have such facilities, but I do not think you are yet ready to handle those."

"You think I'm still squeamish?" I asked.

"Yes."

"I don't know how I can prove that I'm not, if you won't show me anything that might upset me."

"I am also concerned for your wellbeing. Those rooms are dangerous places, and your magical reflexes are not yet sufficiently advanced."

"Oh, come on, you said yourself I was getting a lot better. Only yesterday I turned your attack against you and knocked you off balance. What more do I need to do to convince you?"

Byron looked me over with an appraising eye. "Perhaps I am being too cautious," he agreed. "Let us see how you feel when you confront the realities of our situation."

He led me through a maze of corridors to a door with two guards standing to attention outside. They nodded to Byron, looked suspiciously at me, and then stepped aside to allow us into an enormous room lit by the ceiling above us. Arranged around the walls were three wide, tall archways from which further corridors led away into darkness.

Byron chose the arch on the left and strode towards it. I hurried after him, and as we entered the corridor light surrounded us and lit our way. After twenty yards we reached a large and ancient metal door, intricately carved with protective sigils, almost invisible under the grime of ages. Byron grasped the door's central wheel and with a loud clunk the door gaped open.

Inside lay a simple square room. Floor and walls tiled in gleaming white just like the Divide. There were no breaks in the walls apart from the door we'd entered by, and an identical door on the opposite wall. Byron and I cast no shadows as we entered.

"There's nothing here," I said. "I thought…"

"Have patience." As if on cue, the door opposite swung open. Two nervous men clad entirely in scuffed brown leather wheeled in a covered cage. Their well-padded trousers, jackets and gloves bore scratches and other damage. The thick steel plates that covered their boots were gouged and rusty. The men wore helmets of similarly well-worn steel, with thick leather neck guards behind and clear visors covering their faces.

"You have heard about the Fenrir?" Byron asked as the men positioned the cage in the centre of the room.

"Is that what's in there?" I failed to keep a tremor from my voice.

"Yes, you wanted something dangerous and this should fit the bill. You would prefer a smaller creature, perhaps? Something less frightening?" He called to the two men. "Perhaps you have a pixie for my colleague instead? Or an imp, we have a few of them somewhere." The men chuckled behind their face-shields, and I forced a laugh.

"No, no, I'm fine," I said. The men pulled the cover off the cage, and I reconsidered. The thick-barred iron cage held a lion-sized creature with long silver fur covering its slender body. Its short square face was bald except for a long beard of the same fur. It stood on short but powerful limbs with huge hairless feet from which long jagged claws protruded. The bars were heavily scraped; this animal had spent a good deal of its time in this cage trying to get out.

"Named for the Norse myth of the wolf who will devour the world," Byron said as the two men withdrew. I took comfort in seeing how hastily they shut the door behind themselves, before I remembered I was locked in with this thing and lacked their protective clothing. "Melodramatic, but not entirely untrue. Now, we should shield ourselves from it, if you would be so kind?"

I set to work on a shielding spell, while Byron offered advice about modifications. He wanted it configured in such a way that we could observe the Fenrir, but that it was unable to see, hear or smell us. I started to produce something I modelled on a one way mirror, but he told me to stop.

"If it sees itself, that will not be productive. They are very territorial creatures and will see their own reflections as a challenge to be overcome. While I have every faith in your ability to protect us, I am unwilling to invite a full assault from such a beast. Now, we ought to be higher up, so if you will allow me..." He concentrated for a moment and then he and I slowly lifted into the air. I prodded around with my cane and, unless I looked down, I could not tell that I wasn't still standing on the tiled floor. When I did, the illusion of standing on thin air was vertigo-inducing. Without prompting, I extended the shield beneath us.

With our preparation complete, Byron spoke into a pocket Scry and the door on the far side of the room opened again. Through it came three confused-looking people dressed in normal clothes, shoved through by the same two men in protective gear that had brought the Fenrir. As soon as they were well clear of the door they retreated and closed it. The two men and one woman looked around themselves in fear and confusion. As soon as they caught sight of the cage, that fear turned to terror. One man froze on the spot. The woman screamed and backed away, while the third figure clawed at the door to try to open it. Their shouts and screams were enough to chill the blood, but I knew there would be worse to come.

Byron motioned with his hand, and the cage unfolded like a flower. The steel sides clanged to the floor, and the Fenrir stepped out, stretched and eyed the three people huddled against the back wall.

Chapter Twenty-Five
A Trusted Friend

Conscious of Byron's eyes upon me, I forced myself not to look away. The Fenrir stalked around the edges of the room, its jaws slathered with spittle. It emitted a low, guttural sound. Magnified by the echoing tiled walls, it sounded like an entire pack of ravenous animals. The sound reached deep into the primal fear we all share: the growl in the night, the unseen beast that lies in wait. If ancient men had heard this sound, little wonder they invented a wolf that could swallow the world.

The people pressed against the walls were silent now, unwilling or unable to cry out, perhaps terrified that any sudden sound might provoke the creature. My jaw was tight and my teeth grinding. I poured more power in to the shield to be sure it held. My fists were clenched, my nails digging into my palms.

I hoped, prayed that it was a test of my skills, that Byron would stop it, order me to attack and take down the Fenrir. But as the seconds ticked by, he made no move to intercede. For a moment I thought of stopping it myself, of placing a shield around them or lifting them out of harm's way. But if I did, then I would lose my chance to find out what Byron and Green had planned. As repugnant, as horrifying as it was, I had to let this happen.

One man moved for the other door. Edging around the walls of the room, he made it around ten steps before the Fenrir's head snapped around to watch him. The woman screamed, then stifled the sound as the beast turned to regard her. The man was almost half way to the door, I willed him to succeed even as I knew that door had been sealed tight too. But then the creature's head snapped back, and in a flash of claws and teeth it was on top of him. He never stood a chance. With his deafening scream cut short, he disappeared behind a fountain of blood. The Fenrir shook its head and bright crimson streaks splashed up the wall beside it. The body of the man fell to the ground with a sickening tearing noise as the flesh of his neck ripped loose.

I had to force myself to breathe. I watched in silent horror as the beast licked its bloodied lips, sniffed once at the corpse at its feet, and turned to face the other two people still rooted where they stood. It watched them for a long second, then crouched and pounced. Too late the man and the woman tried to run, and I closed my eyes, unable to watch. The screams stopped in moments, but I couldn't block out the growls, the sounds of tearing flesh and breaking bones. The smell of the spilled blood reached us, hot and metallic, and I fought back waves of nausea. I became aware the sounds had stopped, save for a slow panting from the creature, and I dared to open my eyes once more.

The reality was even worse than my imagination. The creature paced back and forth, blood dripping from its face and paws. More blood painted the walls, almost to the ceiling. Unidentifiable chunks of meat were dashed about the room, and I tried not to remember that these had been living, breathing people moments before. As I watched, the Fenrir howled once, a piercing wail that chilled me to the bone before it lowered its head and began to feed.

After that, everything was a blur. Somehow Byron's helpers got the Fenrir out of the room. I lowered our vantage point back to the floor, avoiding the viscera his aides were now hosing down a sluice. Despite everything, I must have passed Byron's test, must have responded in the way he hoped, since he said he would expect me the next day to continue training. I staggered through the Divide toward the London office.

Tina would know what to do. That was my only thought as I stumbled through the corridors. It was all well and good my grandfather saying to trust no one, but I needed help. I knew she'd never condone what I'd witnessed, couldn't be a party to it. I just had my doubts she'd listen to me after the way I'd treated her.

And so it proved. She cheerfully called out "come in" when I knocked on the door, but her mood darkened when she saw me.

"Oh. What do you want?" She turned back to her work.

"To apologise and explain," I said.

She snorted.

"No really, I am sorry. I never meant to hurt you, but when I got a chance to see what they were really up to, I had to take it." I shuddered.

"What do you mean, 'what they're really up to'?" she said.

I stammered, unable to get the words out. She turned round to face me.

"You look like you've seen a ghost. What happened?"

"Can we talk?" I asked.

"Isn't that what we're doing now?" she retorted.

"I mean in private."

She muttered under her breath, and a silence fell over us. "What's going on? I thought you were happy for to keep teaching you, but you jumped for the chance to get away," she asked.

I told her about the message from my grandfather, the complete message this time, leaving out nothing. As I expected, she believed none of it.

"You're wrong. The Society is fighting evil!" she said. "You're just upset that your grandfather picked the wrong side."

I shook my head. "I saw things, I promise you. Byron, the what-ever-he-is that's teaching me now, he has a finger cut from some guy that translates his language. There's a room where they're draining creatures of whatever they can use, and trust me it'd be bad enough if they were dumb animals, but they're not, I'm sure of it."

"Even so, we need to stop Olivia and she's throwing these things at us. We need every advantage we can get. I don't condone animal testing, or whatever it was you think you saw, but we need to pick our battles. She's the greater threat here. Once she's dealt with, we can put our house in order."

"You're fine using the results of their experiments and vivisection, as long as you don't have to see it? The ends justify the means?"

"Of course not, but sometimes for the greater good..."

"Oh my God, you even sound like them." I wasn't getting through to her. I swallowed the bile rising in my throat and forced the words out. "There is no 'greater good' here. Three people just died in front of me, ripped to shreds by some horrific beast." I felt sick again and steadied myself on her desk.

"You're serious," Tina breathed. "What they hell would they do that for?"

"That's what I've been trying to find out. My grandfather told me they were experimenting, but not the details. Even with what I've experienced, I'm no closer to working out what their goal is. Olivia said it was something to do with getting power, but I don't see how."

"Can you prove any of this?" she asked.

"Oh, come on, you still don't trust me?" I said.

She raised her eyebrows.

"OK, I've not exactly given you reason to. But what do you expect, a signed confession? Who would you take it to? Green's behind it all, and I don't know who to trust. I'm taking a chance telling you all of this."

"We need evidence, either way. Everyone believes Olivia's the evil one, and if we're ever going to convince people she's not, we need more than your word."

"What's the next move?" I asked.

The following morning I paused before I walked into Byron's office. I leant on my cane, pointing the tiny Scry hidden in the handle at the creatures immobilised on the beds in the lab. Rather than broadcasting live, Tina had rigged this device to record, as we weren't sure if Green still had a trace on me. This evening, Tina would recover the recording and see what I was seeing now. Once I had a few moments of footage, I went through to Byron's office.

He began explaining the plan for the day's activities, but I interrupted him. "I think I need a better understanding of what you're actually trying to do here, after what you showed me yesterday. How about you show me some more of your research?" I asked. "It's interesting work. All the research I've done has been in books, so it's nice to get a fresh approach."

Byron was in an effusive mood and more than happy to talk at length about the experiments he was performing. After the experience the previous day, it was less shocking than on first viewing, but when we came to a few cages in the far corner, my heart leapt into my mouth.

"You have more of those Fenrir?" I asked, waving towards the bars.

"Whatever the field teams capture, they bring to us. We don't always have any immediate use for them." He moved to continue the tour.

"Yes, but why keep them then? They'll need feeding, I assume. Someone has to clean out the cages. It seems a lot of trouble to go to for some unwanted Fae."

"Who said they were unwanted?" he replied. "Now over here we have a fascinating experiment..." and he walked over to another bench. I made sure the hidden Scry got a good view of the cages before I followed him.

Chapter Twenty-Six
A Successful Intrigue

I fidgeted on the stool. After the tour, Byron had insisted on getting in a good day's practice in magical defence and it had exhausted me. My hair was singed, my limbs were battered, and I was wondering how you could tell whether a rib was cracked or just bruised.

"Will you sit still," Tina snapped, as she arranged an odd-looking Scry bowl on the table. Where all the others were brass, ornately moulded and ancient, this one was new, plain and pressed out of aluminium. Tina explained it was a new generation of Scry, which enabled us to see my recording in full colour. "Obviously not a test we can show Mr Green," she'd said, "but if this goes well we might replace the everyday ones. And the miniature version I put in your cane could come in very handy for surveillance."

She removed the tiny gadget from my walking stick and connected it to the new Scry. A thick, clear liquid appeared from nowhere and spread across the face of the dish before turning milk white. A moment later, a blurred view of a corridor rose from the surface. The blur vanished, and the view was sharp for a moment before it lurched and blurred again.

"You walked too fast," Tina said. "We're going to get sick watching this."

"I wanted to get there. I wasn't sure how long the recording would last, and besides you know what a corridor looks like."

As I entered Byron's lab, she gasped. "I had no idea there was somewhere like that! And I've got to slum it over here with all this junk." I'd slowed my pace once I got inside, so Tina could see a good deal of the work going on in the outer lab as I made my way across it. Her intermittent gasps of delight, calls of "Oh, I always wanted one of those" or "I think he's working on a new method to dispel night dwellers" confirmed that she had a good view.

"That's Byron," I pointed out as I neared his desk. While we'd chatted about the day's plans, I'd had an excellent chance to point the Scry at him and Tina stared open-mouthed at the image in the dull metal bowl.

"What *is* he?" she breathed. "I wish we could get sound. What does his voice sound like?"

"I've no idea what he is. It seemed rude to ask. But he has the deepest voice I've ever heard. And perfect English, thanks to that thing." I pointed at the finger on a chain around his throat when he stood in the centre of the image.

"What I wouldn't give to study him," Tina breathed. "And you said he was doing research on us Over There, before they captured him?" I nodded.

Tina's first sight of the back room shocked her. At first the image swam and wobbled, but when I stopped for the first time she had a view of the angled tables and the beings strapped to them. She reeled off the names of half a dozen species, explaining that she'd come across some of them herself, but others she only knew by hearsay or from books. Most of the creatures in that room though were alien to her, she admitted.

"They get the Divide-primer from that one," I said, pointing.

"Wait, that comes from an animal?" she asked. "They told me it was a plant extract and a rare mineral! Are you sure?"

"Positive."

"No one said so many had come through!" she said. "They must have been collecting for years!"

"I asked about that," I said. "Byron told me that room represented the last three to four months. He implied that once they get in there, they don't last very long."

"That's not possible. There've not been that many sightings. I mean, I don't expect to see every report but there's no way they've brought all those back in anything like that time."

"They must do a fair bit off the books then," I said, "because he has creatures to spare. Look, in those cages."

Her face dropped as she recognised the Fenrir. "Oh God," she mumbled.

"That's what he used yesterday," I said, before realising she had paused the image and was staring intently at it. A tear ran down her cheek. "What is it?" I asked.

"My father..." she began. I jumped up to comfort her.

Through barely held tears, she explained that her father had been a member of the Society. "He's the only reason they let me in," she said. "He'd taught me as much magic as he could when I was a kid. So when two 'policemen' came to tell me he was dead, I saw through their spells and realised it hadn't been a car accident. This impressed the Council enough to outweigh their reluctance to hire someone like me. That, and I think the coincidence of the name they'd given him being too good a joke for them to pass up. God knows when he married my mother they loved the irony."

I was at a loss for words. My gaze drifted back to the image on the Scry. "It was one of those…" I started.

"Why would they keep them?" She almost screamed.

"He said they had a purpose. They're not experimenting on them, so it must be something else. He wouldn't tell me, before you ask."

"They're not meant to be… I mean, they can't be… The rules say they're to be killed on sight and he's got three of them roaming around in the bloody lab? What the hell is he doing?"

"He's feeding tourists to them, at the very least. I can't imagine that was just for show. Oh God, what if he just put that entire display on to get to me?" The nausea rose again. Had I doomed those three people?

"It doesn't make sense they'd use them against Olivia. They're insatiable. You can't set one on an enemy and expect them to obey you. They'll turn on you as likely as not, or keep attacking anyone and anything in the area until you bring them down. The only thing that stops them is death. I can't even imagine how they'd capture one, let alone tame it."

"Green's planning to use them for something, we just need to find out what," I said.

A long night of brainstorming fuelled by coffee and Tina's secret stash of chocolate biscuits left us no further forward, and we took stock of our assets. I had some old reports and files that I now suspected were merely the censored tip of the iceberg as far as the Society was concerned. There was a connection to Olivia that I had to wait for her to reach out to me to use. I also had an improving but still basic grasp of magic, and a wonky leg. Tina had a few friends inside the Society she wasn't now sure she could trust. Her knowledge of magic was much better than mine, and she had the key advantage that no one suspected her of being a traitor.

We needed more information. Everything the Society did was on paper, old-fashioned files and folders squirrelled away in cabinets or rooms I hadn't seen. I asked Tina if she had any idea where the central filing area was.

"No, but we know who would..." she answered. "We always ask Marlin for the files we need, and he's the one who brings them too, so if he doesn't fetch them himself he'll be able to tell us who does."

"OK, we'll see if he can help in the morning," I sighed. I stood up, stretched my aching limbs and felt my shoulder crack. I winced at the sound and Tina asked if I was OK.

"Yeah, just stiff and sore," I replied. "At least it wasn't my leg this time. I don't understand why Byron won't let me heal it, or just do it himself if he doesn't trust my self-control."

"That's it!" she cried.

"What is?"

"Trust!"

"You're going to have to explain, Tina. My brain stopped working three espressos ago."

"Byron," she explained, "is bound to know what's going on. He wouldn't tell you why he was holding those Fenrirs, but I can't believe for a second he would do that without knowing himself. He's got to be in on it, hasn't he?"

"With all the nastiest things at his command, Green clearly trusts him."

"And you two get along well enough, all you need to do is keep winning him over. Convince him you're on his side, and you're halfway there already from the sound of it." Her voice had a note of bitterness.

"Hang on, I don't like what he's doing any more than you do."

"I know, but our best shot is if you convince him you do," she said.

"Why not just go straight to Green?" I asked.

"He'd be a harder sell, after you and I snuck around behind his back. He never liked me, even before that. And if your grandfather truly was a defector, Green will be watching you closely for any signs you share his sympathies. Byron's an easier target, he's doing what he's told just like us. You'll have to turn on that irresistible charm. Now it's late, you've got a big day tomorrow, off to bed."

I returned to my lonely room to lie wide awake and regret overdoing the coffee.

Two hours' caffeine-addled sleep was not the best start to winning over Byron. He had to repeat instructions several times before I took them in. My focus was awful and after he'd dodged yet another of my misfired attacks, he rounded on me.

"What is wrong with you today? I was just telling Mr Green what a model student you are. Do not make me change my mind," he cautioned. "I see great things for you."

"What things?" I asked. "You mean I might get involved in the fight? Try to take down Olivia with you?"

He smiled, revealing more of his sharp teeth. "All in good time. For now perhaps, I can find something else for you to do which is less likely to put me in danger."

I spent the rest of the day feeding the animals in the lab and cleaning their cages. The Fenrirs were not among the beasts I saw, but when I asked Byron about them, he just said that they had been moved and refused to be drawn further. I completed the punishment detail and sleep-walked to my bed.

The insistent chime of my Scry woke me and I answered it, trying to ignore the foul taste in my mouth.

"You look exhausted," Tina said. "How did you get on though?"

"How do you have enough energy to sound that excited?" I said.

"Don't change the subject. How's Operation Don Juan going?"

"Don't call it that, please. And not well, I wasn't at my best today." I filled her in on what had happened.

"It might be better to take it slow," she conceded.

"I'm glad you approve. I'm sure the Fenrirs went somewhere else. There was no sign of them or their cages anywhere in the offices."

"Hmm, if we'd put a Scry on one of the cages, we might have been able to watch where they took them," Tina said.

"They'd have spotted it anyhow."

"No one spotted the one you snuck in. Let's try it if any more come in."

"If I say yes, will you let me go to sleep?"

"No. We said we'd talk to Marlin today, so get moving."

CHAPTER TWENTY-SEVEN

A CAREFUL RAID

I'd never seen where Marlin lived. It turned out he had a compact room near to my own, to which Tina led me now. He welcomed us in, and I looked around. I was disappointed to see that his room looked almost identical to my own - except for the cardboard boxes placed in front of the sink, cooker and counter tops to enable him to reach the human-scale kitchen. He offered us coffee, and I gratefully accepted. When he opened the fridge for the milk, I noticed a few objects on the shelves inside, which looked like no food items I'd ever seen before. I wasn't able to ask about them before Tina asked about the files. He was reluctant to tell us anything, even after we got him to understand we weren't asking for any files in particular, but for information about where they were.

"You know about Richard's project," Tina said. "He needs to get a better handle on how things are arranged so he knows what to ask for next, you see."

I appealed to his sense of efficiency. "If I could just see the filing area, then it'd help me be more productive. I'd be sure I was requesting the right things, not wasting time on irrelevant or duplicate information, that sort of thing."

"And I'd go with him so as not to take up any more of your valuable time than was absolutely necessary of course," she said. "I know how busy you are, after all."

"And how vital to the smooth operation of the Society," I said. That was overdoing it, but I smiled innocently at Marlin and waited for his response.

"No."

Tina and I exchanged a despairing glance, then I saw my chance.

"How about an upgrade?" I asked, gesturing at his tiny old television and VCR in one corner. "A proper home cinema setup, perhaps? Blu-Ray and a selection of films, with a nice big flat screen to watch them on?" He considered my offer. "Surround sound?"

"And a popcorn machine," Tina added.

"Very well," he croaked. "Come with me."

I had assumed we'd travel through the Divide, but Marlin took us along a dingy corridor at the far end of the office. Both sides of the passage were plain and unbroken and led to a large wooden door that would have been at home in a cathedral. It stood twice my height and almost as wide as it was tall, the corridor widened out to contain it. My eyes watered when I glanced at the join between the door and the walls.

"It's a portal," Tina whispered. "Like the Divide, but single-destination. I guess it's easier to have a permanent link if it's used that often, saves all that faffing around with powders and things if you're back and forth all the time."

Marlin tapped on the door with his long fingernails and spoke under his breath before grasping a large iron ring as big as his head and twisting it. The door swung open, Marlin stepped through and we followed him.

My head spun, much as it had the first time I'd been through the Divide. I thought I would have been used to it by now, but Tina stumbled too.

"That was a long trip," she breathed. "That much disorientation means we've gone hundreds or even thousands of miles!"

"We could be anywhere. Does the Society have offices elsewhere?"

"I never heard about such a thing. I mean, all our reports are from Britain, but I can't believe it's the only place the Fae come through. There must be equivalent Societies around the world. Oh! Maybe they share an archive?" She looked excited. "Imagine what we might find! Reports of different Fae, perhaps? Or alternative methods of controlling them? New magic?"

"Stay focused, we're just here for 'the project'," I reminded her.

We trod on interlocking flagstones, worn smooth by the passage of countless footsteps. The walls were giant stone blocks, at least as tall as I was, stretching high into the air before curling inward to form a vaulted ceiling at the limit of sight. As usual, there was no visible light source, but the area was better lit than the corridor in the Society we'd just left. Ancient doors appeared on each side every few feet, labelled in various odd-looking symbols and runes. They were indecipherable to me. I glanced at Tina, and she was enrapt. "Can you read them?" I asked.

"Huh? Oh, no, but look! These are in Ogham, that's from 4th century Ireland. This one's Runic and wow, Ancient Greek? They must have collected information from around the world for centuries. Is that Phoenician?" she asked Marlin, who shrugged and carried on walking. "Linear-A? No one even knows how to read that!" I had to drag her away.

At a door labelled 'Faerie Society of Britaine', Marlin stopped and opened the door with another incantation. We stepped into a room at least a hundred feet across, much wider than the gap between doorways should allow. Presumably we'd passed through yet another, shorter range portal.

The room was filled with countless rows of shelves packed with cardboard boxes from floor to ceiling. The aisles stretched off into the distance, the end of the room too far to see through swirls of dust. Light slanted in from overhead skylights.

"How on earth are we going to find anything in here?" I asked. Marlin pointed to a row of cabinets against the back wall, each with dozens of tiny drawers. Tina opened one at random and it was overflowing with index cards, covered in tiny but neat script.

With Marlin's help we got to grips with the indexing. The first few drawers were a meta-index, allowing a search for a major category such as 'creatures', or 'field report' or 'spell development'. That pointed you to another drawer or set of drawers further down the first cabinet. In there you could refine your query further. Had you selected 'creatures' for example, you might have sub-categories based on size, weight, scarcity, abilities, appearance, colour, etc. Once you had narrowed your search, you would find one or more cards detailing the locations of other cards in the remaining cabinets. Each of *those* cards had a summary of the contents of a particular box, along with its location on the shelves that filled the rest of the room. By that straightforward if lengthy process, you could locate a storage box with the files relevant to whatever you had requested.

To test, we went into drawer 1 (labelled A-G) and found the cards for 'Field Reports'. Those allowed us to select the next drawer by deciding on a geographical location, date, time of day, persons involved, creature involved (with cross-references to the 'creature' meta-index) and a host of other options. After a brief discussion we started with the most recent reports and followed the card dated this year to cabinet 73, drawer 19. This in turn directed us to a shelf not too far from the entrance, and a set of newer boxes.

Our next challenge would be to convince Marlin to leave us to our own devices in his domain and I racked my brains for a way to enable us to work in private. I need not have bothered. Tina whispered something to him and he smiled over at me, nodded and left.

"What did you say?" I asked when the door closed behind him.

Tina blushed. "I appealed to his love of romance," she mumbled. Putting aside ideas of our hands meeting over a dusty folder, we set to work.

The first file we opened detailed a mundane field trip. A Fae creature had been sighted in Torbay. Members of the FDS had gone to retrieve it and had brought it back to the offices for study in a cat-carrier engraved with runes of protection to prevent the creature escaping. The second file was much the same as was the third. I was beginning to think we were on the wrong track when Tina let out a cry.

"I found something!" She was holding a typical file folder, but tucked inside was another one which wasn't a standard report. It detailed a trip made without a sighting being reported. Two members of the Society had visited Cheltenham and returned with three Fae, and the report detailed how they'd discovered these creatures.

They'd opened a portal Over There.

As Green had explained it to me, the Society was closing these holes in reality to prevent creatures coming through. I knew from my time with Byron that they often brought creatures in for study instead of exterminating them. Now we had evidence that the FDS was not only seeking out these creatures and bringing them here, but were instead capturing them from their own realm.

The label read 'Retrieval Operation' rather than 'Field Report'. It must have slipped inside another folder and been mis-filed. Now we knew what to look for, we could find more of them.

Box after box of folders outlined excursions to known weak spots where a doorway would be opened, creatures summoned and captured, before the opening was sealed again. In most reports they had summoned something in particular, while in others they'd make do with whatever showed up.

What stopped me in my tracks, however, was the mention of 'the Glasgow vault'. "Do you know of a site there?" I asked Tina. She shook her head.

"I only know about Liverpool, where you've been." she replied. "And London, of course. And this place, now. How many sites do they have?"

Back at the filing cabinets we opened the first drawer and looked for 'Research'. Following that lead to the later drawers, we picked 'Location' and read the card:

London

Birmingham

Glasgow

Leeds

Liverpool

173

"How many Fae would that many sites hold?" I asked.

"Too many," she replied. "They're raising an army. But why?"

"An excellent question," said a familiar voice behind us.

Chapter Twenty-Eight

An Upsetting History

Olivia leant nonchalantly against a shelf. Tina readied herself to attack, but I put my arm up to stop her.

"If she wanted to attack us, she'd have done it while our backs were turned," I said.

"Quite right," Olivia said. "You really should be more careful, anything might happen to you while you're sneaking around."

"How did you get in here?" Tina demanded. "You're being hunted all over the country, you can't just wander in to the FDS!"

"Ah, but I didn't, I wandered into the Archive."

"The other Societies," I guessed. "You got in through one of those?"

Olivia applauded. "Well done young man, I knew you were a smart one. But have you figured out that I'm telling the truth yet?"

"I've not even decided if I forgive you for burning me. They tell me I barely made it!"

"It had to look good, dear. They'd never have trusted you if you just had singed eyebrows and a tan."

"My leg is still a mess!"

"Oh, I wouldn't worry about that, we're not likely to survive. But, if you're going to be a crybaby about it," Olivia grabbed my shoulder. Her power flowed into me, pooling in my damaged limb. After just a few seconds, she let me go again and I lifted my trouser leg. My leg hadn't changed. "Oh dear," she said in surprise. "Looks like I might have overdone it after all."

Any anger I might have felt evaporated as her raw power flowed through me. "I guess that's not why you're here though?"

"No. Can we agree the Society are the evil geniuses I warned you about?" Olivia asked.

"It certainly seems that way," I conceded, and told her what I'd seen.

"They're very naughty boys, my ex-husband and his friends," Olivia said.

I hadn't told Tina about Olivia's relationship to Mr Green. "He never said…" she started.

"No, he wouldn't. How embarrassing for the head of the Society to have his own dearly beloved turn against him. Of course, not many knew we were married. It used to be frowned upon to fraternise with the staff, which just made it more exciting. But you two know all about that!" she cackled. Tina blushed, and I explained that we were not a couple. "If you say so. Let's see if we can work out what your Glorious Leader has been up to, shall we?"

We had hoped Olivia would have insider knowledge of what had been going on, but she couldn't tell us much we hadn't already learned. "Your grandfather and I had some people on the inside who fed me rumours, and I'd discovered some truths before I left the organisation."

"Before you went mad," Tina said.

"Before they drove me mad," Olivia replied. "What did they tell you?"

While we searched, I explained the story I'd been told: that she'd delved too deeply into magic, spent too long looking Over There and gone insane, then started a killing spree and become too dangerous to allow to live. To my surprise, she laughed.

"It seems my husband has been leaving out all sorts of juicy details. Would you like to hear my side of it?"

"We'd like to hear the truth," Tina said, clutching a handful of index cards. "These look useful," she said to me, "I'll go fetch the files they index."

"Oh, it's the truth all right, but I doubt you will believe me," Olivia said. "It looks like we're going to be here a while, so I might as well start at the beginning. Are you sitting comfortably?"

"A friend of the family recruited me when I turned 21, after they noticed signs of my being gifted with magic. I spent a few happy years learning about the Fae and practising all manner of spells. And I had a knack for magic, if I say so myself. I was idealistic — aren't we all at that age? And I thought I was doing good work: saving people from Fae attacks, making the world a safer place. Perhaps I'd even get to use my magical abilities to solve problems facing the real world.

"It wasn't to be. Secrecy was absolute. If word got out about the Fae, there'd be panic. People finding out that magic existed would cause chaos on the streets, and we might even return to the times of witch-burning."

"You know they never burned witches, don't you?" Tina called from the next aisle.

"Hanging, whatever. You get my point," Olivia replied icily. "Whatever the truth of it, I had no chance to turn magic to solving world hunger, or saving the whales, or whatever enraged me in those days. But the work was fascinating, and I convinced myself I was still making a difference, so I stayed.

"Then one day a new man joined, Stephen Green. Oh, he was a handsome devil, I can tell you! Every girl in the place had her eye on him, but it was me he noticed. Believe it or not, I was quite a looker too, in those days.

"It didn't take long before we started sneaking off into empty offices when people weren't looking. We thought we were being so careful, but before long the Council found out. They forced us to choose: either stop seeing each other, or one or both of us would have to leave the Society.

"I couldn't imagine life without Stephen. However, I knew he would never leave. He was working his way up the ranks and so he pressured me to quit. I thought we'd pay lip service to their rules, say we'd split up, but continue seeing each other more carefully than before. He didn't want to take that risk and jeopardise his chances of getting a Council seat. We fought for weeks, him pushing me to withdraw from the Society, and me pushing him to have it all. In the end, that drove us apart. He brushed the whole thing off as if it had been nothing. He made sure from then on we worked in different departments. I liked to pretend he was keeping me at arms length because he cared too much, but I realised he just wanted me gone.

"It devastated me, but I still had my dreams of fixing the world and I threw myself into that. We also kept studying the Fae to see what we might learn from them. They evolved with magic, so they have a lot to teach us."

"Right, Byron told me that humans are limited since magic isn't part of our world," I said.

"Oh, you're working with him?" Olivia asked. "I should have guessed Stephen would put you together. He has a perverse sense of humour sometimes."

"Byron's the one performing the nastier experiments," I said. "You met him?"

"I brought him in! But I'll get to that. First, I need to tell you how Stephen and I ended up back together again."

"He got his Council place and repealed the laws about fraternising?" I guessed.

"It was more complicated than that but yes, he convinced them to allow us to marry on the condition that no one know."

"So all that time..."

"He had been carrying a torch for me. It was so romantic when he finally told me. I had been right, he'd kept us apart to prevent us falling in love again, and how could I not forgive him when he told me that?

"We married in secret and carried on where we left off. We both regretted losing so much time, not least when we discovered we couldn't have children, but we took pleasure in being together again. He earned a seat on the Council, alongside your grandfather and the rest of them, and he started making some changes to the Society. I'd never given up on my plans to help the world with magic. He was sympathetic to my ideas, but first he put me in charge of Fae relations."

"You were communicating with them?" I asked.

"We learned from some of the creatures who'd come through that there existed intelligent beings Over There, just as there were here. I convinced Stephen that the best way to learn anything would be to talk to them rather than kidnap them. He let me visit weak spots and send messages through. At first, it was little better than a message in a bottle. Literally, we'd write a note and seal it inside something, push it through the doorway and wait. It took years to get a response from them, but when we did, we were over the moon. At least until we tried to decipher it. We tried many methods to interpret the replies we got. Eventually one of our brightest magic users found a way to translate, but it wasn't pretty."

I described Byron's amulet.

"Yes, that poor fellow. Every moment of every day babbling non-sense at us, unable to make himself understood. One day he had just suffered enough and slit his wrists. When we found him, the men who picked up his body and took it for burial realised that they understood the notes we'd pinned up around the walls, at least until they washed the blood off their hands. The biggest problem after that proved to be finding people who weren't too squeamish to exploit this new means of communication.

"Now we could study the Fae much more easily, and vice versa. That's how I met Byron. He'd been working at the equivalent of our Society Over There."

"He said he was captured," I said.

"True, we had captured him years before during one of our 'message in a bottle' tests. He'd come through unexpectedly, and we'd had to subdue him. Once we got him back to our labs, we weren't sure he was intelligent as we couldn't understand him — Fae speech doesn't sound like human speech. It was all angry grunts and screams to us. Once we got the translation amulets, it took a lot of work to convince him we'd made an honest mistake, but he agreed to be our liaison with the forces Over There."

"That can't have been easy," I said.

"It wasn't," she admitted. "But I didn't realise that behind the scenes Stephen had made other promises to win him over. For the time being, Byron and I worked together on various projects, and our understanding of the Fae moved on in leaps and bounds."

"I can imagine," I said. "I've seen the type of experiments he's doing."

"You have to believe me, I had nothing to do with anything like that. Not with the intelligent ones. We just talked to them. And the animal types... well, there are animal experiments all over the world with strict controls in place to keep them ethical. I always ensured that we treated our subjects as well as Byron had been, if not better.

"But one of the promises Stephen made to win Byron over was to give him his own secret laboratory, where what they called my 'squeamish nature' wouldn't interfere with their ambitions. For five years we worked together side by side, and all that time he had his chamber of horrors to go back to when he finished working with me."

"How can he experiment on his own kind? I mean you talk about it being like animal experiments, but he had intelligent creatures there too," I shuddered. "How can someone do that?"

"Ever hear of a group of people called the Nazis?" Olivia said. "They did all of that and worse during the War to help their troops in combat. They believed that the people they experimented on were sub-humans, not up to their own high genetic standards, and so they were fair game. As far as I can tell, Byron feels the same way."

"Is that when you left?" I asked.

"No," Olivia replied. "That's when I went to Stephen with what I'd discovered, never suspecting for a second that he had condoned it, let alone arranged it. When he explained it was 'the price of victory' I almost threw up in disgust. It turns out that the suffering of a few Fae creatures did not bother my darling husband. As long as it meant we'd be able to stop them, then it was all fine with him. That was when I realised I'd married a monster."

Chapter Twenty-Nine
A Brutal Scheme

"We had a few arguments in our time," Olivia continued, "but that kicked off the biggest one by a country mile. When we'd both finished, and I realised that I couldn't change his mind, I informed him I would tell the Council what he'd done and turned to leave. The next thing I remember, I was strapped to a bed. The son of a bitch had knocked me out and tied me up, rather than have his plans exposed."

"His own wife?" I cried. Tina peered round the end of the aisle behind Olivia, listening quietly.

"That's when he started to 'teach me a lesson', as he put it. If I loved the Fae so much, I should spend more time with them, on their own turf. Strapped to the bed, my eyes held open, he opened a doorway Over There right in front of me, made me stare into it for hours every day. No doubt you've heard what effect that can have." I nodded. "Add to that visits from curious Fae researchers and whatever beasts might pass through the doorway, none of whom I could understand without a translation amulet, and you can imagine how I fared. Before long I was begging him to let me go whenever he deigned to drop in. The damn coward was too afraid to get his hands dirty. He used his minions to take care of my torture. But he stopped by once a week, just to see if I'd changed my mind yet, or lost it. I still don't know where I got the strength to say no.

"Eventually, my mind just fractured, I suppose. But that freed me, in more ways than one. I no longer cared about Stephen, or what he might do to me. But more importantly, I saw things more clearly than before. Connections between magical ideas came to me with ease. Understanding blossomed where only confusion had festered before. In short, what you might call madness unlocked the whole magical world to me, and I made my escape."

"You really went Over There," I said.

"I did. My bonds were easily broken once I understood how the world fit together, and they'd left a source of power and an escape route right there for me. I don't remember what happened while I was Over There, I've pieced it together from what the Fae have told me since. Some of them captured me and brought me to one of their researchers, someone I'd worked with before. Once I convinced them of what was going on over here, they were horrified. Maybe my madness convinced them I wasn't a part of it, or maybe they remembered how I'd treated them when we'd met before, but they urged me to stop it. They got me back over here and kept me in hiding while I recovered."

"When I got my mind together again, I reached out to some members of the Society I trusted. Your grandfather had already had his own concerns about practices in the FDS. They came to a head when Stephen disbanded the Council and set himself up in charge, so he was one of the first to join me."

"Mr Green told me my grandfather was one of those who imprisoned you," I said.

"He'd guarded the door to my cell, but they had told him I was insane and dangerous, so I didn't blame him. Together we built a group of people inside and outside the Society who wanted to take it down, but we were betrayed. I don't know by whom, but Stephen's goons sent attackers after us. They knew where we would be, and we had no defence against some of the creatures they sent. Their research had paid off, they had the start of their army."

Tina, her hands trembling, interrupted us. "I found something," she choked. While I steered her to a chair, Olivia took the file.

It summarised a plan written by Mr Green, outlining how he intended to unleash a Fae attack in major cities around the country simultaneously. They'd open portals in busy locations and send the most vicious and dangerous Fae through to attack as many people as possible. There were projections of how many would die in the initial attack, how many in the ensuing panic and suggested countermeasures to any strategy attempted by the government to control the situation. Utter terror was the obvious goal of this plan, but nowhere in the summary did it suggest why.

Olivia was the first to speak.

"I never thought he'd…" she began.

"You knew about this?" Tina asked.

Olivia shook her head. "Stephen always shared my desire to put the world to rights, but we never agreed on a method. I thought we should show people a better way, using magic to educate and inform people, show them how to care for each other and the planet, that sort of thing. He said I was naïve, that the quickest way to get the world to come together in a common purpose was to give it an enemy. Something to fight, like the allies against the axis during the War, that would bring out the best in humanity. He believed the Fae could be that threat and unite the entire world in opposition. I always assumed he just meant to let the world discover the existence of the Fae, show them that a threat existed. Now it seems as if he wants to go further."

"Can he do that?" I asked.

"Of course he can, if he's been gathering Fae for years. The ones you've seen are probably just the tip of the iceberg." Olivia replied.

"I told you those Fenrirs were trouble," Tina said. "If he's got anything worse..."

"But how has he convinced everyone to help him?" I asked. "Surely not all the Society can support this plan?"

"Some will," Olivia said, "those who share his ideals. I hope most won't, but they'll follow orders without knowing what he has planned. He doubtless told them they were just doing research."

Tina nodded. "If he sold the idea as setting up defences against the Fae, that'd be clever. He could set up teams to respond to any incursion while all the time he's using it as a Trojan Horse."

That was a chilling idea. "I'm glad you're on our side," I told her. "How do we stop him?"

"Get into those storage locations," Olivia said. "It's not a coincidence that they're in highly populated cities. I imagine the attacks will come from there."

"It looks like London might be a separate facility." Tina had been cross-checking what information was in the files. "With most of our people in the office there it'd make sense to keep the dangerous things elsewhere. It doesn't say where though."

"There's no evidence of creature storage in Liverpool with Byron, either," I said. "Not beyond the ones they're actively using. Perhaps that's somewhere else too?"

"You need their trust," Olivia said. "They will not tell you anything until they're sure you're on their side."

"You're not going to burn him again, are you?" Tina clenched her fists.

Olivia laughed. "Stand down, young lady. It's up to him now." Turning to me she added, "Are you up to it? You'll have to be very convincing if you want to learn more. My husband and his friends won't trust you unless you're willing to do whatever they want."

"I'll do it," I said with feigned confidence.

"We can't rely on you alone," Tina said. "Sorry, but we need a backup plan. I've been working on those tiny Scrys and I can ensure they're not detected. If you plant a couple of them on cages, we might learn something about the Vaults' locations."

"Either way I need to be in Byron's good books," I said. No more hesitation, no half measures.

I would have to bury my squeamishness and play the part of a willing co-conspirator.

Chapter Thirty

A Subtle Rumour

The next day brought a message from Byron. It said he had been unavoidably detained by vital business and wished me to continue with my own studies until further notice.

I spent the entire day berating myself. My reaction to the Fenrir might have given me away, or perhaps my poor performance on our last meeting had given Byron reason to reconsider his mentorship. Maybe he'd got wind of our trip to the Archives. I tried to distract myself from my failure by returning to my scanning and research.

I read papers until my eyes hurt, stared at the laptop screen until I gave myself a headache, and drank too much coffee.

By evening I was pacing my office, swearing about a lousy long-dead magician who had left vague yet tantalising hints about a spell he'd developed to find hidden Fae. I had started reading hoping it might be useful for locating the Vaults. But his flowery language and tendency to mask his words so that no one else might discover his secret were the final straw. I flung the pages away and watched in horror as my office door opened and Tina walked in. The combined research notes of Richard Phelan, 1820-1876, whistled by her head.

"Charming," she deadpanned. "Am I to assume that you're not thrilled with the results of your research?" She dismissed my mortified apologies and took in the scattered papers, countless coffee mugs and my dishevelled appearance. "You need a break, something to eat, and something to drink that won't increase your blood pressure to dangerous levels. Come with me." I followed, trying to explain my searches so far, but she cut me off with an imprecation to "not talk shop". Chastened, I asked instead where we were going.

"It's a surprise," was all she would say. I followed her along familiar corridors and then realised where we were headed.

"Your lab?" I asked, puzzled. "Surely you're not going to start teaching me again?"

"And risk the wrath of Byron? No, this is a social call." She pushed open the door to her laboratory and ushered me inside.

The usual debris and clutter had been swept off one end of a lab bench to make way for a chequered tablecloth. On it stood white bone china plates, silver cutlery and two crystal goblets. On a small trolley to one side was a large domed silver platter. A smell of roasted meat displaced the usual scents of bleach and incense. Marlin stood beside the table, a folded towel over his arm, pouring wine from an old bottle.

"You made me dinner?" I gasped.

"What? No, Marlin did!" she replied, blushing. "I mean, I thought you needed a distraction, and something to eat. Marlin set it all up." He beamed proudly. Tina whispered to me. "I had to draw the line at candles though." She looked pink around the ears. I thanked both her and Marlin profusely.

Marlin bowed. "Try it first, this is more complicated than tea."

I smiled. "If it tastes as good as it smells, you have a wonderful career ahead of you."

It did. Marlin had made a delicious goulash with hearty dumplings, soft noodles and a tray of steamed vegetables which improved my mood after just a few mouthfuls. The wine was ancient, and so rich and smooth it was like drinking velvet. I couldn't remember the last time I'd eaten so well, and it was exactly what I'd needed.

"To Marlin!" we toasted as he cleared away the dishes, and for a few moments my worries faded. Surely we'd be able to locate the hidden Vaults and put a stop to Green's scheme. Then once again the enormity of the task before us overwhelmed me, and I sagged on my stool.

Tina put down her glass, rounded the table and put an arm around me. Instinctively, I stiffened.

"OK, what's going on? Am I that repulsive?" she asked.

"No, not at all, it's just..." I started.

"Was it an affair? That 'bad decision' you talked about, is that why Claire wants a divorce?"

I shook my head. "I wish it was. I saved her life." I took a gulp of my wine and explained. "She was pregnant, a boy. The morning sickness had been so bad, I'd had to take some time off work to look after her, but then things got better. Until I got a call one day." I sighed. "Something had gone wrong, and by the time I got to the hospital she'd lost so much blood... I kept asking what was happening, what I should do, and the doctors kept asking me to decide. I wanted them to ask her, to wake her up and ask her, but they couldn't. It was all on me."

Tina's eyes filled with tears, but she didn't speak.

"I told them to save her, save Claire. As soon as I'd said it they pushed me out of the room, set to work. The next thing I remember was seeing little George in an incubator. He was so small, so tiny…"

"I'm sorry," Tina said.

"They said it was too soon, that I'd given him a chance at least, but…" I swallowed hard. "She said I should have chosen him, not her. I said I couldn't bear to let a machine keep her blood pumping if she was gone, and…" I buried my face in my hands. Tina put her arm around me again, and this time I didn't push her away.

"Do you really think they will do it?" I asked. "Attack all those people and hope it brings us together?"

Tina shrugged. "God knows if it'll work or not, but they're willing to try. But we're going to stop them." She reached across the table and took my hand in hers. I looked up into her eyes, brimming with tears. "Aren't we?"

I gripped her hand tight. "We're going to try."

Dessert was apple pie laced with cinnamon. We barely tasted it.

It was three torturous days before Byron sent word for me to return. Despite my concern that I'd lost his trust, he greeted me as if nothing had happened. While I continued my lessons and worked to wheedle more information out of him, Tina was seeing if we had any allies amongst the regular staff. It was delicate work trying to sound out people's genuine beliefs and allegiances when we weren't sure what they knew about the Society's true purpose and plans. Tina and I re-grouped over coffee one day and discussed our approach.

"Byron's still not opening up, and I don't want to push him too hard," I said. "I know the clock's ticking but it's risky drawing attention to myself like that."

"It's the same for me," Tina replied. "I have to beat around the bush so much I can't tell if people don't know anything or simply don't understand what I'm asking."

"What if we don't try to sound people out?" I suggested. "How about instead we get Green to do it for us?"

Tina choked on her drink. "Sure, why not?" Her tone became sarcastic. "'Hi there, we're working to bring you down and we wondered if you could just make a list of your enemies so we can ally with them?'"

"Haha, but I'm serious. We start some rumours, referring to what looks like a planned attack from Over There. Perhaps the creatures they're all out trapping are scouts or even raiding parties preparing the ground for a full assault? Once the rumour mill gets grinding on that idea, Green will have to speak up. After all, his lie and the truth both rely on the Society being on the front lines of the defence, to be the cavalry riding to the rescue of humanity."

Tina nodded. "That's not a terrible idea, actually. There're already rumours about increased Fae activity, so we can just exaggerate them. That way we won't have to stick our heads up and risk discovery. Plus, once the rumours are flowing, no one remembers who started them."

"And then we can ask him to help us all prepare for the coming battle. We'll have everyone pre-warned, and even pre-armed. We don't need to seek out the army we need, we make it."

"I'll mention it to the few I know I can trust so far," Tina said. "But how will we get the message out more widely?"

"I have an idea on that front," I smiled.

Tina and I prepared several fake documents discussing the increase in Fae activity, dropping hints at a coming attack while stating nothing overtly; tantalising clues were much better. The more puzzle pieces we spread around, the more people would have to talk to join them up, and the more widely our story would spread. Some of our forgeries were back-dated to suggest the increasing Fae problems had been covered up for a while, but the Council were getting more and more nervous about 'something big' coming. We seeded the bluntest references to key individuals big on speculation and gossip, while the hints and comments that were innocuous enough on their own, but bolstered the narrative when seen in context, went to a wider audience.

We agreed to start small, with a few subtle hints dropped into field reports and see whether that was enough to gain traction. Only a few days after we started, Tina dashed into my office and closed the door behind her.

"What's up?" I asked as she shrouded us with a silence spell.

"Mary just told me that pixie captures are up 75% this month!" she squealed.

"OK?"

"We didn't mention pixies in our misinformation," she explained, "let alone that large a rise. Besides, I've checked the field reports: they're not even 5% up."

I still wasn't sure what she was getting at.

"Has Marlin been slipping you decaf? The rumours have a life of their own! People are inventing them all by themselves. I think we'll be OK, if people are this primed to believe and even exaggerate what's going on, it won't take much!"

Chapter Thirty-One

A Vicious Menagerie

We stepped up the campaign, and the stories spread even wider and faster than we hoped. Every day we met up after my sessions with Byron to compare notes. Rumours of something big were spreading, and even those who never listened to the office chit-chat were whispering to one another.

"Byron's furious," I told her one evening. "He thought there was a leak in the inner circle for a while, but the more outlandish rumours seem to have persuaded him otherwise. He figures that if someone were telling outsiders about his plans, they'd be a lot better informed."

"Let me guess, you had something to do with him reaching that conclusion?" Tina smiled.

I grinned back. "I may have, but it's still driving him crazy. Any idea how much longer before Green feels the need to speak up?"

Tina nodded. "I spoke to him a couple of hours ago and he mentioned something about addressing misconceptions."

"I hope he's not just going to deny everything," I said.

"Don't worry," Tina touched my arm. "The second management deny something, that proves it's true. Didn't you ever work in an office?"

Green issued a memo the next day denying the rumours. Just as

Tina predicted, the denial stoked the flames higher. Within two days we overheard people openly discussing 'the coming fight' in the corridors.

The last stage was for us to visit Green. We outlined the rumours we'd heard, expressing our anxiety about this unchecked fear in the Society's ranks. He waved us to silence.

"I know what people are saying," he groaned. "I've tried to correct them but they just keep believing."

"We have an idea," Tina said. Green looked up with hope in his eyes. "All these rumours spring from fear. People can't see what's coming."

"Nothing's coming!" Green said.

Tina nodded. "Of course we know that, but if you set up some simple defence training, perhaps people would feel better prepared and stop worrying so much?"

"No," Green said. "If I train people to fight a threat I say doesn't exist, how does that make me look?"

"Like a concerned leader," I said. "This will show you have their best interests and safety at heart."

"Nonsense, I'll just look incompetent."

"Right now people are scared, and they think you don't care. You've dismissed their worries, and they feel let down. It won't take much to reassure them."

Green slumped in his chair. "Very well. Ms Black, set it up. Gather a few of your colleagues and set up some classes. After hours, mind you. Work's being disrupted enough already with this nonsense. I'll issue a memo later." Tina smiled, we thanked Green and turned to leave. "Richard, might I have a moment please," Green said.

With a worried glance at me, Tina left. As the door closed behind her, Green rose from his seat.

"You and I know the truth, there are more creatures out there than usual. You've seen a few of them in Liverpool. But the Fae are not planning any orchestrated attack."

"How can you be so sure, though?" I asked. "And how can we convince people? That's the reason Tina and I came to see you, to defuse the tension this is all causing. Why not just tell them?" I understood why not, but I was curious what his answer would be.

"Because we are planning one," he said.

My look of incredulity was genuine. "An attack? On — on the Fae?"

"Of course," he replied. "That's why we're stockpiling those creatures, to fight fire with fire."

Byron was in a foul mood the next morning when I arrived. He was pacing around the labs so fast the furniture rattled.

"That bloody idiot," he exploded. "Offering defensive classes like that."

"He's just trying to deal with the rumours," I said. "And he explained to me that the plan is to attack the Fae, so surely the more hands the better?"

Byron stopped his pacing. "Even now he suspects you might not have the stomach for it. But I know you are ready to hear everything."

"What else is there to tell?" I asked.

"We will indeed be combating Fae beasts," Byron said, "but I can tell you that this attack is not our true purpose. The Society is not what it once was, as you have no doubt noticed. The perils of living in secret, you see. It was once supported by rich benefactors, men who fancied themselves explorers of the occult. They were the face of the Society as a foolish club for men who believed in goblins and gnomes. They paid their dues and swapped stories about fairies at the bottom of the garden. Those few allowed to witness the truth paid richly for that privilege. It worked well, yielding plentiful funds and support in high places, but none of the attention that such activities might have brought.

"Much of this was before my time," he explained. "When I arrived, this period was already ending. Science and technology had long turned the minds of men against us, and only children believed. Those few illustrious families that once supported and nurtured Green's forebears petered out. Bloodlines lost or broken, sons failing to follow in the footsteps of their fathers. Now we live by constrained means. We lack the funds to do as we wish, the patronage to elevate our struggle to its rightful place, and the time has come to make a drastic change in our fortunes."

"But what does this attack on the Fae have to do with it?" I asked. "It seems like a huge expenditure of time and energy for something so unpredictable."

He smiled. "Ah, but it will not be unpredictable, you see. We will attack the Fae, yes, we will defeat them, but we will not wait for the bedraggled wildings to rise up. We will begin the fight on both sides and step out of the shadows."

"You're engineering a war? You intend to release those creatures and then clean up the mess you made?" He nodded. "Just to restore the fortunes of the Society?"

Byron frowned. I had to be careful.

"Wow, that's clever!" I said. "I get that Green wants respect, power. But what about you? Something tells me that with Fae attacking on all sides, you're unlikely to be welcomed in the corridors of power. No offence, but you're not exactly unthreatening."

Another booming laugh escaped Byron. "I do not seek the limelight, I have my own goals. And, as the power behind the scenes, I would be much freer. Something Green still does not realise, despite leading the Society for so many years. One of many things. But come, it is time for you to see our preparations."

The Vault was within the same building as the labs in which I'd been training. Part way along one corridor was a simple wooden door I must have walked past a dozen times without noticing it. Even looking straight at it, my attention slid away. Now I'd been led directly in front of it, I tried to examine it but kept losing concentration. With an effort of will I saw it was magically warded with glowing sigils etched in the ancient wood, before I lost interest again. Whatever was behind here was something the Society didn't want anyone stumbling across.

With a complicated gesture, Byron opened the door onto another short corridor with an identical door a few paces away. Another complex hand gesture locked the door behind us, opened the other, and we stepped towards the Vault. Moments later, the room spun around me as I took in the scene.

Imagine a concert hall or a cathedral, so immense in every direction that you could almost see the earth curving away from you. Now tile it in bright white, light it from one of the Society's invisible sources that cast no shadows. Finally, fill it with aisle after aisle of cages. Some were stacked five or six deep with walkways in front while others were a single cage, tall enough to reach the distant ceiling. All were made from the thickest steel with magical wards on their bars. I was glad that from my current vantage point I could only see into a few of them. There was a mix of the terrible Fae I'd glimpsed so far and other, yet more frightening creatures.

People roamed the various catwalks, shrunk into ants by the distance. Closer up, scientists and technicians were inspecting and checking the creatures. Older, tired-looking magic users stood in each aisle, I assumed for protection.

Or perhaps as decoys? I remembered without mirth the joke about the guy who tells his friend he can't outrun a lion, but gets the reply "I only have to outrun you..."

The nearest aisle was five cages high and stretched into the distance. I tried to figure out how many there could be. Call it three hundred on each level with five levels, 1,500 cages... and there were over a dozen aisles stretched out in each direction.

"I think he finds it amusing," Byron rumbled beside me, shocking me from my thoughts. "Green. He calls them our 'little cages'."

"Right..." I stammered. "These are the small ones? Don't tell me there's any bigger than that!" I pointed at an example two aisles to my right, which dwarfed its neighbours.

His deep, booming laugh rang out. "No, any bigger and we would truly struggle to contain them," he chuckled, and I prayed he was telling the truth.

As he walked off along the aisle I hung back for a moment. I slipped one of Tina's miniaturised 'Spy-Scry' devices out of my pocket and attached it to one of the cages before hurrying to catch up. This room alone held tens of thousands of creatures which, if the cages were anything to go by, were at least the size of the Fenrir I'd watched kill three people in mere seconds.

And they had five sites.

"Why so many?" I asked, my hands rattling my teacup in its saucer. After strolling through the aisles, we'd come back to Byron's office, where their own equivalent of Marlin had left a pot of tea and two cups. "Surely it's dangerous, keeping all your eggs in one basket. Or all your Fenrir in one dog house."

Byron chuckled. "Nothing can get through those doors without the proper ability, and the inner door cannot open until we seal the outer one. We have the same arrangement in our other 'baskets', do not worry about that."

"There are more storage areas? So many of those cages were full, I was going to ask what happened when you ran out of space."

"We can confine as many as we need."

"Sure, but what if someone sabotaged the wards? Olivia might try something, and I bet she's thought of turning your own monsters on you."

"We have considered that," he agreed. "And yes, we can seal off that room with everything inside it. Permanently."

"Including your people?" I asked.

"If necessary," Byron said.

I shuddered and drank more of my cooling tea. "And you plan to release these creatures, to create panic and mayhem? How exactly?"

"We shall open portals inside each of the Vaults. The other end of these portals will be distributed so as to span the entire country. When we release the Fae from their cages and encourage them through the portals, they will appear everywhere simultaneously." He spoke calmly, as if he wasn't discussing the deaths of thousands, maybe millions. I could barely keep my face from betraying the turmoil inside me.

"And then what?" I asked.

"And then we wait."

"What?" I gasped.

"If we put down the creatures too quickly, it would not only appear suspicious but would diminish the effect." Green's plan had a terrible logic. If you're going to pretend to be the saviours of humanity, you'd better make sure humanity really needs saving first.

I continued to probe Byron for more details. The idea was as terrifying as it was well-thought-out. Green had drawn up lists of targets, casually determining which locations would provoke the greatest public outrage or fear, which would lead to the greatest casualties and even considered the best time of day to attack.

The sole good news I discovered was that only three of the Vaults were in use, and not all five. The attacks would be launched from London, Liverpool and Glasgow.

I showed a new determination in my lessons that day, something Byron attributed to my understanding the true purpose of our activities. He sensed I was keen to be in the attack's vanguard and determined to prove myself to earn that honour. I knew my only chance at disrupting the plan would be if I was on the front lines.

Chapter Thirty-Two
A Reluctant Agreement

Back in Tina's lab under the security of a muting spell, I brought her up to date.

"There's no way we'd be able to fight them out in the wild, even if we could identify and recruit everyone not already involved!" she said.

"That's the idea. Byron said that even if they dedicated everyone in the Society to stopping the attacks, they couldn't do it. But the plan is they'll focus their combat efforts on high profile places. They'll protect city centres, government buildings, schools and so on, while elsewhere there will be plenty of casualties. This way people see the horrors they are being saved from. It's no use to Green if in two weeks' time everyone just remembers a few big dogs that needed putting down."

Tina gasped. "How can you be so calm? Do you even hear what you're saying?"

"Of course I do." I sighed. "I've had to spend all day pretending to be impressed. If I appeared squeamish at the thought of casualties, they'd stop telling me anything on the spot. But I have to admit they have planned extremely well. By ensuring they defend the government, they can get a seat at the table when it's all over. Green has his eye on a new Department for Fae Affairs, or something similar. And by protecting schools they can appear decent family-loving people, willing to sacrifice themselves for the next generation."

"That's something, at least, if they're not targeting kids…" Tina saw my expression. "Oh no, tell me they're not…"

I nodded. "Some of them will get through. They count on the deaths of children provoking an outcry. There'll be demands to protect them, and no-one will refuse Green his post."

"Bastards!" Tina shouted. She shook in her seat, her knuckles white around her coffee cup.

"Look, we always knew there'd be killing," I reminded her. "And we always knew they were bastards too. We need a plan. If they can close off the Vault then so can we, right?"

"It'd only be locked from the inside. I can't think of any way to entomb an area with the resources of the Society dedicated to finding a way in," Tina replied.

"What about sending the creatures back Over There?" I asked.

Tina rolled her eyes. "That'd weaken the barrier, open even more instabilities and blow up in our faces."

"Let's release them into the Vault," I said. "If there's a mass breakout, that's exactly what they're trying to protect against. We just open the cages and let them lock it down."

"And anyone inside would just open portals right away and send them all out. If someone trapped me in there with those things, that's the first idea I'd have. Then we're right back where we started. Worse, with none of Green's men ready to fight."

"Wouldn't the lockdown prevent portals being opened? That's a big flaw in their protection if the Fae can still get out."

"That's only a flaw from our perspective. It's designed to prevent the creatures from getting loose in the Society, and that's all Green cares about."

"Can *we* block them from creating portals?" I asked.

"Maybe." Tina grabbed a book from a shelf nearby and flicked through it while I waited impatiently. "Yes! Here we go. Warding against portals." She skimmed the text. "It explains how to set up protection against anyone opening a doorway in or out of a space, but it's difficult."

"OK, so we trigger the locks, trap them all inside and open the cages. Give them a taste of their own damn medicine."

Tina looked at me, shocked.

"On top of everything I've seen, if they're going to target children, I'm not giving them a second bloody thought."

"We still need to find the Vaults," Tina said. "The portal blocking spell has to be cast from outside the area it's containing and it'll be short range."

"That Scry I hid might help us with Liverpool, but I'd need to visit the other sites to do the same. I reckon they're underground, there're no windows anywhere like there are here."

"You work on that, we must strike them all at the same time or lose the element of surprise. But we don't have anyone we trust enough yet. And we have to hit three locations simultaneously."

"We've got Olivia," I reminded her.

"She's the most wanted woman in the world right now. Plus we don't have any way to reach her, and she's not what I'd call stable."

"The only other way to stop this is to attack the head of the serpent," I said, "and we're not strong enough to take on Green ourselves. We'd need her either way."

Tina shook her head. "Even if I was sure I could trust her, it'd be asking too much to expect her to kill her own husband. You heard their love story. No, we know where we need to strike. If we don't stop them before they open those portals, there's nothing we can do to prevent a catastrophe. We have to destroy those Vaults."

Chapter Thirty-Three

A Tentative Hope

Since Byron had mentioned portals the previous day, I wanted him to show me how to create one myself. If I was going to prevent this attack, I needed to see what I was up against.

"I feel I'd be able to help you better," I said, "if I could understand each stage of the process. You've been doing a great job teaching me to attack and defend, but I want to know everything."

"I have people who will open the portals for us," he said. "Do not forget that they will be in the room when the creatures emerge from their cages. They will be in more danger there than fighting with us."

"Of course, I want to be on the front lines," I said. "But even there it might be helpful to open portals, to slip a beast behind a locked door for example." I squashed down my disgust at the idea and tried to present the image of a loyal foot-soldier. "And surely the more different fields of magic I study, the better I'll become at any of them."

"Maybe you should use that silver tongue of yours instead of magic," Byron laughed. "But very well, I will show you."

As I gathered my energies, I recited the words he gave me. As always they tried to slip from my mind as I spoke them, but I was getting better at remembering them long enough to complete a spell. I had to focus on the location I wanted to travel to, picture it as completely as I could. You needed to be very familiar with the place you wanted to reach, and the more familiar and closer the place was, the easier the spell would be. Reluctantly setting aside any ideas of zipping to the Bahamas for lunch, I tried to decide on a location.

"For now, try with your eyes open," Byron advised. "You are learning so much in one go, this will be easier if you can see your destination until you get used to controlling the energies." He indicated the far corner of the room. "Go there." I started to walk, and he laughed. "I meant, open a door to there," he said.

Embarrassed, I refocused and stared into the opposite corner. I pictured a tunnel through the air between myself and that spot, said the words and pushed my energy outwards. A swirling black vortex appeared in front of me, sucking in all light in a space a foot across. A matching one swirled in the other direction at the far side of the room. "Hold it there," Byron said, and threw a pencil into the spiral.

With a loud bang, it exited the other portal and buried half its length in the wall opposite.

"Stop pushing," Byron said. "You are sending energy into your portal, and that power has to go somewhere." I adjusted my mental image to stop the flow of magic, and the portals wobbled and shrank. "Not all of it," he said, "just enough to keep the path open." I nodded and stabilised the holes. He tried again and this time the pencil came out of the other portal at the same speed as it went in, but its yellow paint was charred and the wood beneath was blackened and smoking.

I needed many more attempts before I could send something through without it either catching fire or smashing against the far wall. Byron then told me to try on a living subject and brought in a few small Fae to practise with.

My nerves got the better of me on my first attempt and the creature was unrecognisable when it exited the portal. The next couple arrived intact, though dead.

Byron saw my despair. "Remember how you pulled the energy from them before, you can visualise that now, yes?" I nodded. "Monitor that life force, if it falters you can support it like a drunkard stumbling."

I opened the portal once more, and this time followed the silver thread of the thing's life through the doorway. To my delight it was unaffected by the journey, and I regathered my energies, more optimistic than I had been in days.

Tina's work had also borne fruit. She was ready to teach me a way to prevent portal opening in any confined space.

"It's very simple," she said, "when you open a portal you're bending space and time, creating what scientists call a wormhole. Imagine a piece of paper, and you want to get from one edge to the other. Instead of going across the face of the sheet, you roll it up and step over."

"OK," I said. "You set up a shortcut, right?"

"Pretty much," she replied. "To prevent someone doing that you just need to stiffen space-time."

"Right, you lost me there. What was that now?"

Tina smiled. "Unlike paper, bending the universe is really hard. Physicists think you need massive gravitational objects like planets and stars to make a bend noticeable and if you want to open a wormhole, you need negative energy or some other exotic matter."

"Nope, still lost."

"Just trust that it's hard to do. Magic makes things easier but think of it like pressing on a weak spot. Or better yet, like using a lever to move something."

"Magic is a crowbar?" I asked.

"More or less. And if you can't wedge it in a crack somewhere, you can't lever it. So all we need to do is smooth over the cracks. Metaphorically."

She assured me the exact method for doing this was not as hard as understanding the principle, but I still wasn't able to grasp the technique.

"It's already applied all over this building, unlike Liverpool. We have the Divide to keep comings and goings constrained. What if you can spot the traces of the spell? That might help you understand."

I focused and examined the thin silver strands of magic around me. Being in the heart of a magical office building meant that there were thousands of them, but I had learned to ignore most of them during my various training sessions. *This* one was a binding spell to hold the cages shut in the lab. *That* one was a Scry call in progress. An interrupted, tarnished-looking thread was Mrs Orange looking for her keys again. One by one I picked up each thread and examined them, releasing them again when I knew they weren't what I was looking for.

After a few minutes, I was getting nowhere. "I can't seem to see it," I admitted. "Every thread I follow goes back to someone or something specific, there's nothing I can find."

"Focus less," Tina advised. "Chances are it'll be spread thin so if you look too close you might miss it."

"Not seeing the wood for the trees, eh? OK." I closed my eyes and stretched out my magical senses, trying to take in the whole lab, the entire office in one go. Something glinted in the corner of my perception, but when I looked again, it slipped away. "Hold on," I said, and I shifted my attention to focus without 'looking' directly at it.

Like one of those pictures that seems to be random noise, but when you cross your eyes enough resolves into a three-dimensional image, it snapped into focus. A gossamer silver sheet wrapped the entire building, clinging to the exterior walls, invisible unless you knew it was there. Now I'd spotted it, I could trace the spell around the offices, see the dent formed by the Divide. As I watched, someone must have been entering as the dent deepened, tore open and snapped back, completing the barrier once more.

I probed at the spell, picking a spot near our lab, and got a feel for how it moved, how it reacted. Touching magic like this was always a confusion of senses. Taste, smell, touch rolled into one. But like any sensory experience, this was unique, as different from my magical shield as a toffee apple from a bookcase.

Now I knew what I was seeing, I understood. Once more I sensed that magical knowledge slip into my mind without conscious thought. Now I tried to connect my new knowledge to what Tina had explained, but her metaphor was only a first approximation to the truth. Magic had no relation to human understanding, I knew that, but I had never appreciated what that meant. Magic wasn't just inexplicable, it couldn't be understood in human terms. Imagine trying to describe the colour green to someone who had never seen it, and you get a vague idea of the problem.

I let the images fade. "I get it," I said. "I think I really get it."

"A touch over-dramatic," Tina smiled, "but I'm glad we got there, eventually."

I shook my head. "Not just the block, I understand magic. Something clicked, and it makes sense to me. Watch." I made a gesture, muttered the words (the right ones, they had to be perfect), and a glowing copper shield appeared between Tina and I. Unlike the ones I'd conjured before this one was bright and solid, crackling with power and a faint scent of electricity mixed with roses.

Tina reached out and touched the shield, arcs of gold shooting across its surface from her fingertips. She pushed against it, gently at first and then harder, but it didn't flex. She stood back and readied a magical attack. With a nod, I told her I was ready.

The shield absorbed it. I sensed the power she'd put into her attack break across it like water on a beach, then travel along the line, joining the disc to my hand and re-energise me. She gasped. I dissolved the shield with a thought and grinned at her. "See?"

"How the…" she started, then shook her head. "You can't…" she tried again. "What the hell?" she finally managed.

Chapter Thirty-Four

A Magical Search

Magic was like riding a bike. Once you had the hang of balancing, pushing off, steering, if your balance was good enough you could learn to ride without touching the handlebars, or pull wheelies. I'd taken off the training wheels.

Tina and I left the office via the Divide. In an empty car park outside Newport, she challenged me to one magical test after another. We started with the shield which she bombarded with countless attacks to no avail. Then she raised a shield of her own and asked me to attack her.

"Are you sure you'll be safe?" I asked, concerned if my newfound power overwhelmed her defences.

"I'll be fine, thank you," she replied, sticking her tongue out at me.

She was. Despite my best efforts, nothing I threw at her buckled her shield. After a few minutes, she called a halt.

"OK, now try levitating," she said. I strained, visualising myself lifting from the ground. I recalled Byron's elevating us both before the Fenrir attack and tried to focus on the magical effect and not the circumstances. My feet remained stuck to the ground.

Whatever else Tina asked me to do, I failed at unless I'd already been shown how to perform the spell or it was an obvious extension of something I knew.

"So you can't just do any magic you wish, you still need to learn how," she stated after a few botched spells. "That's a relief! I mean it'd be handy for our purposes if you were a walking nuclear bomb, but you can see how that might not be reassuring."

"I need to know how a spell works before I can do it, yeah. With the shield you'd been teaching me that for so long I found obvious ways to extend it."

"What about the portal blocking? You seemed to understand that from observation... but I've not taught you. Want to try?" She opened a portal across the car park and kicked a discarded drinks can through before closing it again. "Try to stop me," she grinned.

I shut my eyes and pictured a silvery sheet around her side of the car park, pulling it tight to the walls, ceiling and floor. Opening my eyes, I was pleased to see nothing was visible, but I could still catch glimpses of it when I extended my senses. "Give that a try," I told Tina.

The smile on her face vanished. She extended her arms, muttered under her breath and her forehead furrowed with concentration. After a few moments she gasped for air, and I realised she'd been straining hard. "OK, you got me," she admitted. "It's like there's nowhere to put that crowbar."

"I didn't feel a thing," I said. "I thought it'd tug at me when you tried but there was nothing."

"Outstanding," she said. "You can zip up the Vaults and make sure those creatures don't get out. Should we block Scry activity too? Do you suppose that's possible?" Tina asked. "That way they can't even warn people about what's happening, or call for help."

I thought for a moment. "It ought to be possible, but they use Scrys all the time. Chances are they'd miss the portal block since they won't be opening any. I mean, it's hard to detect unless you know what you're looking for, but cutting the phone lines would alert them to our interfering."

"Quite right," said Olivia behind us. "You really need to watch your backs. For supposedly secret agents, you're not good at it."

"How the hell did you find us?" I asked.

"Tina here invited me," she replied. "She claims to have something to help us stay in touch. But I didn't see any evidence my husband was following you. And it took me a while to lose my own watchers. Don't worry," she added, "I didn't hurt them."

"You had a way to communicate with her?" I asked.

Tina shook her head. "I used her idea of putting messages in bottles. I sent out a few notes to places she's been, carefully coded so no-one else would read them. I'm glad you found one."

We walked to a local cafe where we filled Olivia in on what we'd discovered. My ability to deconstruct a spell and do it myself impressed her, though she didn't understand how I did it. My comparison to recreating a recipe from tasting a dish didn't help.

"I got my own grasp of magic by very different means. Your grandfather would have understood, I'm sure," she sighed. "I think he had some similar talents, though he either wasn't as capable or was reluctant to show off like you."

Tina explained our plan, and Olivia approved. "When is it happening, though?" she asked.

"We don't know," I admitted. "It must be soon though, those cages are practically full. I need to get into the last two sites and plant Scrys so we can locate them. Oh, speaking of which..." She handed us each shallow palm-sized brass bowls with ornate patterning around the edges where it flared out. Olivia turned hers over in her hands and whistled.

"Where did you get that idea?" she asked, impressed. I inspected my own and detected a vague glimmering of magic which vanished as soon as I thought I saw it. Each time I searched for the signs of a spell, it slipped out of my sight again.

"Frequency-hopping?" I guessed, and Tina nodded.

"It's a similar principle, yes. No one magical connection is held for long enough to trace, before it jumps to a new one. It won't keep us from being overheard for very long, but might give us a chance to send an urgent message."

"Should save me having to put myself at risk again," Olivia said.

"Or us," I pointed out. "If they realise we're talking to you."

"Right, that too," she added.

I was right, the plan was getting close to fruition. Green called me in for a meeting the next day. He informed me they had enough creatures available now to be confident their attacks would gain the attention they wanted, but still be able to bring them under control, eventually.

"That's great," I said. "I'd like to take a look. Just to get a sense of the scale of it, if you think it's OK."

For a heart-stopping moment I thought he would refuse. "I have some business in Glasgow, you may accompany me if you are curious." I fingered the spy-scry in my pocket as he primed the Divide, and we stepped through to an office identical to Liverpool except for the colour of the walls. Liverpool was papered in a faded green and Glasgow was a faded reddish brown that now resembled nothing so much as dried blood. I pushed down the thought and sent out my senses.

No barriers. Just as with the Liverpool site, there were no wards preventing a portal being opened, and the same was true all the way to the Vault itself. So far, so good. If we could secure both sites, we'd have no problems trapping the creatures inside.

Green introduced me to Mr Lime, who was in charge of the assault from Glasgow. Another old man, tall and unbent with an impenetrable accent. I suspected he dyed his hair as it was darker than mine, but not his handlebar moustache, which was a striking silver scar across the centre of his face.

The Vault was the same as the previous one, with the same Fae in familiar looking cages. I stepped beside a cage and peered inside. While Green's attention was elsewhere, I carefully reached as far down the side as I could and attached the Scry to one of the bars out of sight. "And London's the same?" I asked, as casually as my pounding heart allowed. "Or is that different because it's attached to the main offices?"

"Who told you that?" Green asked, amusement in his voice.

"I just assumed... you have a separate location then?" I asked.

Another nod. "But yes, it's the same as this one. Nothing exciting to see."

As we headed back to the Divide, I grabbed a note from one of the desks and stuffed it into my pocket.

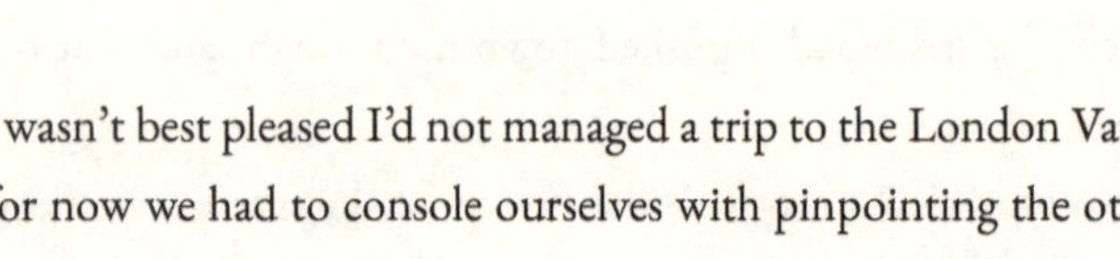

Tina wasn't best pleased I'd not managed a trip to the London Vault, but for now we had to console ourselves with pinpointing the other two sites. Armed with Ordnance Survey Explorer Map 275 (Liverpool) I locked myself in my office. I opened a Scry connection to the first of my hidden spy devices and watched the oblivious people come and go for a moment. I smoothed the map out over the top of my own Scry, pulling it taut with a heavy book on each edge. A candle burned on the desk in front of me, and I used it to melt a few drops of red wax in a thimble-sized cup I held in tweezers.

I concentrated on the spell Tina had shown me, reciting the unfamiliar words, focusing my energies on the cup. The molten wax began slowly rising as a tiny pulsating ball glistening in the candlelight. I scowled with the effort of concentration as it moved about six inches above the map, forward and back, left and right. I felt a pull and let it follow, gliding to a spot on the far left of the map sheet, where it circled over a few inches of paper. With a deep breath, I exerted one last push of energy. The wax formed into a needle and plunged towards the map. When it hit, it splashed, covering an area about half-an-inch across. I relaxed, my back aching with the sudden release of tension, and leaned in to see more closely.

At the scale of the map, that wax blot covered about a quarter of a mile in each direction. It lacked the precision of a GPS fix, but was more than enough for our purposes. The Vault was somewhere in or near Bootle, on the banks of the Mersey. If we centred our search there, it shouldn't be too tricky to scan that area magically for the precise location.

It was the work of a few minutes to determine that the Glasgow Vault was also on the outskirts of its namesake town, near Clydebank, across the river from the airport. I'd not heard a plane while I'd been there, so I assumed this building and its Liverpool counterpart were deep underground.

Via the secret Scry I filled Olivia in with our findings so far and asked her if she had any idea how to find the London Vaults. She said she would ask someone who might know and asked for time to find them.

Time was something of which we had very little. We needed to launch our attacks as soon as possible, and without notice if we got wind that the release of the creatures from the Vaults was imminent.

"If we neutralised two out of three, that at least would be something," I admitted, "but if we can't get into the London one the damage will still be done. We absolutely have to find it, and fast."

"Leave it to me," Olivia assured me.

I was passing my discoveries on to Tina later that day when the regular Scry on her desk rang with a new and deeper tone than I had heard from it until then. Before she could even grasp the edges to answer it, it filled with the black fluid and a distraught voice issued from it.

"Healers to the Divide."

We were on our way to the door before the fluid had drained away. Whatever was happening was not part of the plan. Surely they hadn't triggered the attack already? Surely we'd still have time. We arrived to find a small group crowded around the reception desk, as two elderly magic users cradled Mr Red between them out of the white-tiled arrival room.

His impeccable suit was burned and torn, his hair scorched. He'd lost a shoe, and blood stained his pristine white shirt. Too much blood. Most surprisingly, he was crying.

Two more people helped him to stumble along the hallway, the crowd parting around them. As he passed me he lifted his head, tears leaving lines across his blood— and soot—covered cheeks. "She's dead," he wailed, before he was urged back into movement.

Who was dead? Not Olivia, if he'd killed her then he'd be jubilant. My answer came as four more figures stepped out of the Divide, carrying a body between them on a blanket.

Chapter Thirty-Five

A Risky Excursion

Mrs Orange.

I wish I could say she looked peaceful. I wish I could say she looked to be sleeping, but the terror and pain on her face would not allow it. The long gashes covering her arms and legs and across her torso were deep and angry red, while the rest of her skin visible through the tattered remains of her clothes was pale as the room she'd just been brought through. I realised where the blood soaking Mr Red's own clothes had come from. Why hadn't they covered her up? Why had they not given her even a modicum of dignity in death?

I understood when Mr Green stepped through behind her, anger, sadness and defiance on his face. He wanted us to see her that way, wanted us angry and fearful. This was to be the trigger for everything that was to follow.

"It was Olivia," he said. Over the gasps and cries from the crowd, he continued. "She ambushed Red and Orange, trapped him and made him watch as she tortured..." his voice broke.

"What did she want?" I asked, afraid of the answer I knew was coming.

"The Vault locations," he said. Damn her, now they'd ramp up the defences on all sites. I was surprised that my anger was stronger at her blowing our cover, than her having killed to get the information.

"What do we do?" I asked, as Byron hurried along the corridor towards us. Green hustled us into his office and closed the door.

"We move up the plan. The attack will be at dawn. "

Tina and I would have to move fast and regrouped in her lab.

"How could she do that to her?" Tina sniffed back tears. "Of all the people..."

"Mrs Orange had been here forever, knew everyone, knew everything, and was a lot more talkative than everyone else I've met."

"She didn't talk though," she said. "He did."

Now that we had the locations of the Vaults, we needed to visit them in person. We had to see and memorise a nearby location to be able to open our own portals out of the Vaults, and it had to be close enough that we could then extend our blocking spell back inside. It was no good opening a portal back home, for example, as we'd be too far away to block the creatures' escape.

I knocked up a couple of fake sighting reports and went to see Green. He was so overworked that when I offered to go and check them out to save anyone else the bother, he didn't even ask where we were going.

Tina and I used the Divide to travel. I'd picked locations far enough away from the Vaults to ease suspicion if anyone were watching us. We completed our journey on a rattling two-carriage train on the way to Liverpool. Seeing the people on the train going about their every day business — kids on the way home from school, folks with shopping bags and briefcases — reminded us of the stakes of the upcoming conflict.

"We'll do it," Tina reassured me, squeezing my hand.

"I hope so." A shiver ran down my spine as I recalled the sound of tearing flesh. I swallowed hard. "I should check with Olivia, find out where the London Vault is."

Tina rounded on me. "You think I want her help now?" she hissed. "You still think she's got anyone's wellbeing in mind, after this?"

"I'm not going to make excuses for her, but if she knows where that Vault is we can stop anyone else from dying."

"She's blown the whole damn thing."

"They're attacking soon," I told her. "They believe she's working alone and she can't attack more than one site, so they're going on as planned. We all need to strike together."

"I still don't like it," Tina said, pulling the new Scry from her jacket pocket. I snatched it from her hand.

"You're not the best person to talk to her," I said.

Olivia's face appeared in the black surface. "What the hell were you thinking?" I asked her.

Her voice echoed inside my head. "You said it was vital that we found the location, so I did. If you're going to be squeamish about my methods, you need to be clearer in your communication."

"Don't try to push this onto me. Where is the last Vault? At least tell me you found out."

"Of course I did, but we can't talk like this. Someone might overhear. I'll deal with it, don't you worry."

My protests didn't dissuade her, and she severed the link.

"Olivia's going to cover the London Vault," I said. "I tried, but she refused to tell me where it was, so we have no choice but to leave it to her. I'll take Liverpool, you take Glasgow. We'll attack at 11pm. Green's planning to launch his assault just before dawn, so we should have time."

The spot marked on the map was a crossroads in a residential area, terraced houses stretching off along each street and a Chinese restaurant on the corner. I was examining the map again when Tina grabbed my arm and pointed.

Olivia Street, the sign embedded in the wall said.

"Just a coincidence, I'm sure," I said. "Let's get started, we're very conspicuous and we don't look like lost tourists."

Tina muttered a spell under her breath and stabbed an arm out. "That way," she said, pointing towards a line of trees at the end of the road.

We passed a boarded up pub at odds with the well cared-for houses, and in less than a few hundred yards we'd reached the edge of a park. Large steel gates barred the road, but a pedestrian entrance allowed us access. Now we were less conspicuous among dog walkers, kids in pushchairs, and people making their way home across the grass. Tina once again whispered her incantation and led us to a small mound left of the entrance. The path split and passed around both sides of it, and it was ignored by the locals. No kids played on it, no adults glanced at it, even the dogs didn't sniff at it.

"Here." Tina pointed to the ground. I stretched my magical senses and half-felt, half-saw an enormous cavern deep below. I focused gently and carefully so as not to set off any traps and brought the image clearer. Sure enough, it was the Vault. The grassy mound of earth sat right on top of the cage room, while the offices extended under the park toward where a hum of traffic suggested a major road.

"I think from anywhere in this park it'd be easy enough to enclose the Vault and the office," I said. Tina and I both looked around us to memorise the sights, sounds and smells of the place so either of us could manage to open a portal back there later. The goal was to step from the Vault itself to this park, then slam the doors shut behind.

Just to be safe, we also formed memories of the nearest station. It was a small, regional one and somewhere we felt confident we could arrive without drawing attention. I picked up a few discarded tickets from the entrance to allow us to use the Divide, to give us another alternative.

Back at the office we half-expected to be grabbed, accused or led away, but no-one yet suspected we were up to no good. We headed straight off towards Glasgow and the other Vault.

The wax spot had been more or less centred over the Clydebank Museum. Once there, Tina guided us again until we reached a spot near a sizeable college building. In the same space were a business park and a leisure centre, but behind that was a small grassy patch fenced off and unused. Surrounded by modern buildings, it was unusual not to be built on, and I wondered if despite the Vaults being underground the Society still shielded them from curiosity. It wouldn't help to have someone driving foundations through your office space or storage for dangerous creatures, no matter how deep you buried them.

I scouted out the underground structure and determined that the offices were under the grassy square, but the Vault itself stretched under the River Clyde.

"Will that be a problem?" Tina asked, "Running water can sometimes interfere with magical energy."

I shook my head. "You can follow the tunnels and lock it off from here."

Once more we memorised the place, and a location inside the leisure centre too. I found two receipts on a table in the cafe and pocketed them. Back in the office, I handed her the note I had pocketed earlier to let her prime the Divide for Glasgow. I grasped her hand as she took it. "We're going to win this."

Byron had been looking for me. I managed to convince him I had been tying up some loose ends prior to the attack, readying myself for what was to come. We travelled together to Liverpool to prepare for the following morning.

"Do you really think Olivia will try anything?" I asked. I wondered what his opinion of her chances were.

"We are not concerned," he said. "As long as she is alone, she is essentially harmless. Whatever trouble she causes will most certainly not stop us, and we intend to blame her for everything, anyway. So a little extra chaos will not matter."

"Blame her for it? But how?" I asked.

"Green will use his new position of authority on, shall we say, supernatural matters to identify her as the mastermind of the attacks. She will become the most wanted terrorist in history. With the whole country out for her blood, I do not expect it will take long for the authorities to track her down and eliminate her."

"Clever," I admitted. "If anyone sees her fighting, they'll just assume she was on the wrong side anyway once the dust settles. And she's not likely to surrender and tell her side of the story, she'll just attack if she's cornered."

"Exactly. Now, rest and prepare yourself for what is to come."

Rest was something I couldn't do, but I could prepare. I drew a little power from several creatures in the Vault as I waited. I would need every bit of energy available. As I roamed the aisles of the Vault, I identified the nastiest of the creatures, the ones most likely to inflict harm, and memorised their cage's locations. I didn't wish to linger there any longer than necessary and returned to a quiet corner of the offices to try to relax.

At quarter to eleven I called Tina on the regular Scry from the office in Liverpool. We had worked out a simple code in case someone overheard us.

"Fancy something to eat?" I asked.

"Sure, tapas sound good?" This meant she was about to leave for Glasgow. Chinese would have meant she was unable to get away, Indian that they had discovered us.

Olivia wouldn't answer the secret Scry. She'd promised she'd do her part, and as reluctant as I was to trust her, I had no choice.

With a minute to go, I walked into the Vault room and took a last look around at the rows of cages. Even this last time, the sheer strangeness of the creatures still gave me a moment's pause.

11pm.

With a final check that no-one was watching me, I opened a portal and stepped through, appearing by the small grassy mound in the park. The few people still around at this time of day didn't appear to have noticed my sudden appearance from thin air. I focused my energies, expanded my will, and created the blocking spell around the room beneath. Once that was secure, I extended the invisible shield to enclose the entire Vault, offices and all. No alarms sounded, no-one reacted. With a muttered prayer I reached out my mind again and probed at the door to the Divide. A gentle pressure in the right place and... It disconnected, and I had the strangest sensation, as if a loose tooth had come free of its socket.

Now the alarms sounded. Low chimes rang from every Scry in the place, and a confused voice issuing from them announced that the Divide was unreachable.

And that's when I opened the cages.

CHAPTER THIRTY-SIX

A DEADLY ATTACK

No-one noticed as I mentally reached out and unlatched each of the cages in rapid succession. Not until the doors swung open and confusion turned to panic.

I tightened the portal blocking spell I was casting and steeled myself for the chaos. I couldn't look away, I had to be sure that none of these creatures escaped. And a part of me wanted to watch the destruction these people had worked towards being visited upon themselves. Hesitant from being caged so long, the first of the creatures jumped down from its open cage. I took slight satisfaction from noting it was a Fenrir.

The Fenrir looked around before charging towards the nearest human. He'd attempted to raise his own shield when the doors opened, but I pulled a little of his power away from him. I took just enough to weaken his defences, but not enough that someone would notice me doing it. The beast didn't slow as it ploughed through the shield and sank its teeth deep into the man behind. Trying to ignore the sickening crunch of bone, I turned my attention away to see what else was happening.

By now more of the Fae had left their cages and were joining in the fighting. Some stalked the people trying to flee, but many fought among themselves. Where possible, I reached out and forced the larger of them apart, encouraged them to go after the people instead. The smaller creatures I left to their own devices.

I sensed a few portals being attempted, but none of them strained my ability to stop them. A small group of people had gathered at the Divide door, hammering on it and trying to open an exit. No-one appeared able to reconnect it, but I steered a particularly nasty-looking beast along the corridor towards them. They raised shields in a wall between themselves and its hungry gaze. Just for a moment I let them think they were safe, before I drained their power to reinforce my own spells. They fled, it chased them, and killed the first two with swipes of powerful clawed feet. One brave man turned and readied an attack, firing lightning bolts at it. His surprise when they appeared to ricochet off its skin did not last long before it was upon him. It was over in seconds.

By now half the monstrous things in that Vault lay dead. Most had fallen to the larger of their number, but a few had been felled by resistance from the humans still alive. A barricade had been erected while I was busy at the Divide. A jumble of shield spells, furniture and doors pulled from their hinges blocked the main corridor. The humans cowered behind it, trying to open portals. One had a Scry which he was using to call for help, though none could come soon enough. I disconnected the call with a thought, anyway.

I easily drained the shields, but it was hard work to magically move the physical blockage without losing my grip on the blocking spell. I settled on starting a fire at the very heart of the piled up wood, fanning the flames to grow it as fast as possible before someone realised. Distracted by their escape attempts, by the time they realised their barrier was on fire, it was too late to put it out and they had to retreat. Some braver creatures tried to clamber over the burning wreckage and suffered for their efforts. One or two could fly and swooped down on the fleeing figures out of the smoke. Before long the flames had died down enough for the rest of the Fae to make it through, and that small group of men was no more.

I couldn't check in with Tina until I was sure I had secured the site. I didn't know how long it might be before the last person capable of opening an exit portal would be... no longer able. When I focused my attention to the other rooms for a second, I felt rather than heard the screams and withdrew again with a shudder.

By now, Green had to know what we'd done. I glanced at my watch — five minutes. Was that all it had been? Even so, losing connection to all the Vaults at once would have been noticed immediately, and I could expect them to reconnect them before too long. Or would they come and investigate some other way? I looked around myself nervously, in case there were people there ready to take me down. No-one was in sight, and I let out the breath I'd been holding.

Had I trapped Byron in the office with the others? My route to the Vault hadn't passed his office, and I'd not dared check magically before I had my spell in place in case he detected me looking for him. I checked the spaces beneath me once more.

His magical signature, so familiar from our training sessions, was nowhere to be seen. I focused more carefully and probed the office from end to end.

Only two people were still alive, and they had shut themselves in an office and barred the door. Both were human, so I left them for now and checked for Fae signs. Most of the creatures had fallen to their cage-mates or the staff's disjointed defence, and those that remained were fighting among themselves. No sign of Byron, which meant that either he was dead, or had not been there when I sealed off the rooms. I moved on, checking each bloodied face in turn for his demonic appearance.

He wasn't there.

Damn it, he must have been with Green when I'd started this. Now it was time to end it. I turned my focus back on the two survivors. They were trying to break my portal blocking spell while reinforcing the hasty assemblage of furniture piled against the door of their office. I contracted the bubble of magic I'd created around the offices, herding the surviving Fae towards them. A Fenrir was already launching itself at their door, baying for blood, and I could see the splintering wood would not hold for long. I extended my will one last time and with effort collapsed the barricade, allowing the creatures in.

It was over in moments — they never stood a chance — and then I could reabsorb the power I'd used and shut off my spells. I pulled energy from the surviving Fae to charge up as much as possible. Those few that remained I drained with small satisfaction until everything in the Vault was dead.

The Scry chimed softly in my pocket.

"It's done," Tina told me, sounding as rattled as I was. I told her I'd dealt with my site. "Any word from *her* yet?" she asked.

"No, but it's only been a minute," I reminded her. "I'll call you back soon." I hung up and called Olivia.

No reply.

It would need all three of us to return to London and face Green together. Tina and I hadn't thought we could take him down alone, and Byron might well be with him. Olivia might have been busy, she might have been ignoring me. Or she might be dead.

I called Olivia again and again, but no reply. She'd had more than enough time to complete her task, and I was getting worried. I called Tina back.

When she answered, her voice was shaking so much it even sounded broken via the telepathy of the Scry. I heard her spit a few times and wondered if she'd thrown up. I certainly felt like it.

"Are you OK?" I asked.

"Uh-huh," she replied, "yes. It was just... horrible."

"I can't get hold of Olivia," I said. "I think we need to head back to London, see what we can find out before we're missed." Tina made a gurgling sound I took for agreement and I told her to take her time to feel better. There was no point turning up and immediately being suspected. "Don't just use the Divide from where you are, open a portal somewhere else. If they can trace where we came from..."

I opened a portal back to the park near my house — the furthest I'd done so far — and then used the Divide to return to the offices.

Chaos greeted me. Someone jostled me aside as they re-primed the Divide and a team of six dashed through. I walked into reception and asked Janice what had happened.

"Olivia, that's what," she replied between Scry calls. "She's attacked, killed dozens!" She returned to her work, and I headed at a run to Green's office. Even before I reached the door, his and Byron's voices were audible, raised in argument. I slowed my pace to listen.

"Where is she now?" Green shouted. "Even if you didn't see this coming, I can't believe you let her escape again!" So she'd made it out alive.

Byron's voice rattled the glass in the office door, but his tone was measured. "I knew she would try something, but she had help to strike all three Vaults at once. You did not find the spies in your own house, do not blame this on me."

I closed the distance to the office door and burst in.

"I just heard," I panted. "What the hell happened?"

For a second, they just stared at me. They must have assumed I'd perished in Liverpool with the others. Then Byron narrowed his eyes and regarded me critically.

I had a story prepared. "With the attack planned for tonight I wanted to make sure my wife was safe, so I went to set a few wards. They're saying Olivia attacked?"

"All three Vaults have been wiped out," Green said. "An orchestrated attack, which means she has allies."

"Wiped out?" I gasped. "But..."

Green stood behind his desk and wiped his forehead with a handkerchief. "She somehow cut off the offices from the Divide, that was the first we knew of it. Normal procedure is to restore the connection from their end, but they could not. Likewise, we couldn't reconnect from here either."

"Open a portal," I suggested.

"They were also blocked until a few minutes ago. Someone has gone through now though, and... it's not pretty," Green continued. Byron was still staring at me, and I shifted under his gaze. "There are a handful of creatures left in one Vault, but they're sated now, no use for an attack. And besides, we've lost so many people we would struggle to contain them."

I tried to ignore Byron's stare and ask what I'd be expected to. "She's escaped? And her accomplices? Did anyone see who they were?"

Green shook his head. "No survivors mean no witnesses, but I don't think we've seen the last of her. If I were her I'd be looking to finish the job."

Byron spoke for the first time since I'd entered the room. "Where were you?" he asked, his eyes still fixed on me.

"I told you, I went home," I fought to keep my voice calm. "I got back about two minutes before I came running in here." A lengthy silence stretched between us, but I fought the urge to fill it. The more information I volunteered, the guiltier I'd look.

"When did you leave Liverpool?" he asked, stepping closer to me.

"I'm not sure, maybe 10:30?" I said. "No, later, quarter to eleven?"

"By the Divide?"

"Err, no." I looked at my shoes in a show of embarrassment. "I used a portal, I thought it'd be quicker, and I wanted to see how strong I was getting." Byron was close enough now that the urge to step back was almost too strong to resist. I was sure his eyes had never left me. "Where were *you*?" I asked, with a bravado I didn't feel.

Finally, he blinked.

"Weren't you in Liverpool too? How did you escape if the Divide and portals were blocked?" I forced myself to lock eyes with him even as his rank breath ruffled my hair. After an eternity, he stepped back and looked over at Green.

"I do not have to defend myself."

"Really? Why not? It seems as if everyone is under suspicion," I replied.

"Because I know it was you," he said flatly.

I laughed. I should have been terrified, should have launched into denials, protested my innocence, even launched an attack, but my instinct was to laugh in his face. This was evidently not what he expected either.

"I hope you have some evidence for that," Green stepped around the desk to stand beside us. "That's a very serious accusation."

"Oh I do. Regard his aura," Byron replied, his eyes boring into me. So that was what he'd been doing. "It is that of the Fae."

I'd recharged from the creatures before coming back. They said the best lie was always the one nearest the truth. "Of course it is, I needed the boost to get home, it's a long way. I just borrowed a little to make sure I had the strength, like you taught me."

Byron stepped forward again, his eyes inches from mine and his nose all but poking me in the face.

"Liar."

Chapter Thirty-Seven

A Fatal Moment

My blood ran cold, but I gathered my energies and threw my shield up just in time to deflect Byron's blast, fiery energies rebounding around Green's office and scorching the wallpaper.

Tina crashed through the door with a shield already raised, and I backed up alongside her, walling ourselves off behind our shields as we inched backwards, Byron's fury unleashed. He looked more animal, more Fae, more *other* than I'd ever seen him before.

"Explain yourself," Green barked, and it took me an instant to realise he was talking to Byron.

"These two worked with your wife to undermine us. They are behind this attack." He glared at us, but did not launch another attack. "I can prove it, too," he added. He produced one of the tiny Scrys we'd planted in the Vaults, and I groaned. "Yes, it was particularly satisfying to use your own tools against you." He grinned and gestured at the Scry on Green's desk.

The bowl filled and produced its image — Tina in the Vault in Glasgow. This would be damning enough on its own as she shouldn't even have known of its existence, but then the cage doors springing open and her disappearance through a hastily conjured portal removed any doubt. The image swam, and my attack played out.

I didn't wait any longer and speared a jolt of power through my shield straight at Green. He knocked it aside, his own invisible shield already in position. Again and again I lanced out bolts of energy, trying to find a weakness, a gap in his defence, and every time he deflected me. I reabsorbed what energy I could and tried another approach.

Reaching my focus behind him, I pulled free a handful of heavy books from a shelf above his head. They hung in the air for an instant before I flung them as hard as I could at Green's back. The assault momentarily distracted his attention, and his shield flickered in my mind's eye as he ducked and swung it around to deflect the books.

"Now!" I called to Tina. We struck hard, Tina adding her own power to mine. A stunning blow fractured Green's remaining shield and caused him to stagger back, losing balance. We pressed home the advantage and threw everything we had straight at him.

But Byron blocked us both. He effortlessly threw his own protection in front of Green, and our blasts ricocheted around the office. Tina flinched behind her shield, but I concentrated on capturing the spent energy. This battle was far from over.

With our shields up, we were at a stalemate. Byron lobbed a few blasts at us, which we diverted and partially absorbed, and whatever we tossed at him or Green was similarly pointless.

"Where is she?" I hissed at Tina. "We need her to tip the balance." Tina shrugged. While there was still frantic activity outside the office, it lacked the note of panic which her sudden arrival would no doubt have caused.

Time for a distraction. "We know what you're up to," Tina said, her voice quavering but her gaze fixed on Green. "I mean obviously we do, but we've stopped it," she added.

"What kind of sick monster wants to kill so many people just for power? A seat at the table?" I asked him. "And did you really think you'd be able to get away with it, blame it all on your wife? With so many people in on it, you'd be blackmailed for the rest of your life."

"I had plans for that," Green began, but Byron interrupted him.

"Enough!" he shouted. "You think you are so damnably clever, do you not? You do not understand the machinations in place."

Green looked as confused as Tina and I. He stepped away from Byron, as if to get a better look at his colleague.

"What are you saying?" he asked.

"I played you all against one another, kept you all busy and ignorant, the way you humans always are." Byron looked pleased with himself. "You," he said, pointing at me, "think Green is seeking power for its own ends. And you..." Tina flinched as his long finger aimed at her face. "Think you are better than him, but wrongfully ignored. While he..." A dismissive wave over his shoulder at Green. "Always thought he was in charge. But Men can only go so far. And this one has come to the end of his usefulness."

We'd been fighting the wrong enemy.

The news of his betrayal struck Green hard, his shield sagging as he reeled and steadied himself on the desk. No, it was more than that - something was weakening him. He doubled over, grunting in pain, and his shield vanished. With my magical sense I saw pulse after pulse of silvery energy leaving his body and flowing into Byron's outstretched hand as he drained the man of power and life.

Green withered and shrank, his skin greying and wrinkling before our eyes. His back bent and his limbs twisted as he moaned in agony. His clothes hung loose as he struggled to raise his head, to meet Byron's disinterested gaze.

"Why?" he croaked, his voice almost inaudible.

"Revenge," Byron replied. "You snatched me up, drained me, probed me, tortured me, kept me caged and alone. You took what you did not and could not understand, and you abused it. Your actions have weakened my home, killed so many of my kind and all to further your own goals. No more." Sadness tinged his fury.

"No," gasped Green, as he collapsed to the floor, his arm clutching at the desk for support it couldn't find. "No." Then he was gone. A dusty, shrivelled shell of a man remained, a bundle of sticks tossed aside.

I strengthened the shield in front of me. Tina did the same, her panting breaths audible over my own thudding heartbeat. I knew from my lessons that I couldn't defeat Byron alone, had never got past his defences. Now, with Green's power added to his own, he might well be unstoppable even for two of us. I readied my energy nonetheless, determined to go down fighting if I had no other choice. I extended my senses, searching for another source of power to draw on should I need it. Tina's own energies glowed brightly beside me, and I felt a few sparks from the people outside the door... For a moment, nobody moved.

Then Byron tipped his head back and roared, shattering the glass in the door behind us. Shouts and screams came from the corridor as sharp fragments flew in all directions. Tina and I flinched, distracted at the crucial moment. But no attack came. Byron lowered his eyes to meet ours and regarded us for an eternity.

"What now?" I asked. Still he just stared, the slightest movement of his eyes to flick between Tina and I. Should we strike? Could we even hope to slow him down? If we had Olivia...

"Now I go," he said.

"Back Over There?" Tina asked. "Back... home?" He shook his head.

"No. Green's infernal meddling has weakened my world too much, I must make a new home for my kind."

"You're not finished, are you?" I asked, knowing the answer. "That was your real plan for the creatures in the vaults. You're going to turn this world into your new kingdom, an alternative world for the Fae."

"Yes."

"Then we have to stop you," I raised my arms, and saw Tina do the same from the corner of my eye.

Byron regarded us sadly. "Do you remember when I showed you the Vaults?" I nodded. "Your reaction was one of anguish. You felt sorrow for the creatures we had enslaved, even the dumb beasts I worked with. You heard about my ill-treatment and you sympathised with me, you viewed me as a being deserving of respect and kindness. I believe you recognised something of yourself in us."

"What do you mean?" I asked. "I felt sympathy, yes, but I'm nothing like you."

"Do you not wonder why your power is so strong? How you can bend magic to your will so easily? You know that magic is not a part of this world's evolution, that only the Fae can truly wield it. So why do you think you can? A part of you is like us."

"I'm part Fae?" My legs wobbled beneath me. If he struck me now, I wouldn't be able to defend myself. "That's impossible, that's nonsense."

"Somewhere in your ancestry is a changeling, one of us exchanged for one of you. This is why I spare you now. Do not do something foolish to make me change my mind."

"I can't let you wipe out humanity!" I protested. "Nobody out there had anything to do with what happened to you, it was Green. And you've got your revenge."

He shook his head again. "We must take what we need. I am sorry, Richard."

And then he vanished.

I reached out to see if I could still detect him. He was gone, I was sure. Not invisible, not hiding, but gone.

"How the hell did he do that?" I asked, to no reply from Tina. "You can't open portals in here, we tried."

"Evidently he can," Tina said. "Or it was something else entirely. Maybe that's why he needed the extra power." We looked at Green's remains and sighed. "We have to find him."

The corridor had cleared after Byron had shattered the glass, but people still peered around corners from a safe distance. We pushed past them, brushing aside their questions. Explanations would have to wait.

We reached the Divide before realising we didn't know where we should go. Olivia finally answered the Scry on our third try. Not knowing what to tell her, we settled for a meeting at my house and promised to bring her up to speed then.

The moment we stepped out of the Divide, I opened a portal —

no sense in hiding the location now — and we arrived in the street outside my house. I half-hoped to see Claire waiting for me. Instead, Olivia stood in the doorway to my home. Tina looked to be preparing to attack her until I stepped between them.

"Where have you been?" I asked. "We've been trying to reach you. We heard you destroyed the London Vault but..."

"What happened to my husband?" Olivia asked. She visibly sagged when we didn't answer.

"It was Byron," I began, but Olivia didn't hear. I was astonished to realise she was crying. Tina relaxed her posture slightly, her anger ebbing as she saw a woman in the depths of grief in place of the monster she had expected.

Olivia wiped her eyes. "Sorry. Even after everything he's done, I still..." she choked again, and bit her lip. "Anyway, at least he's not a threat to us now." I led her into the living room to sit. Tina, her anger buried if not abated, went into the kitchen to make tea. By the time she brought it back out, Olivia was back to her old self again, if red around the eyes.

I explained what we'd learned: how Byron had always been the power behind the scenes, and his plans to create his kind a new home here in our world.

"We need to find him, before he can do any more harm," I finished. "Where might he go?"

Olivia thought for a while before replying. "One of the other sites, I expect," she said. "Not much point going back to the Vaults now. If he can even reconnect them to the Divide, there aren't any Fae left to use."

"I thought they weren't using the others?" I asked.

"If Byron was plotting against Green, he might well have had a backup Green didn't know about, some creatures to use against him..."

"Where?" Tina asked.

"I'm not sure," Olivia said, "but there were two more mentioned in those files you found. And I have the locations." My stomach tightened as I remembered how she'd extracted that information. Tina's fists clenched in her lap, and I spoke quickly.

"It'll take all of us to bring him down, if we even can. We stick together," I said, "If we don't find him at the first site, we all go to the second." I expected Olivia to argue, or just vanish in front of us without a word, but she nodded.

"Birmingham first. Shall we go?"

CHAPTER THIRTY-EIGHT

A FRANTIC SEARCH

We stepped through Olivia's portal and found ourselves in Birmingham city centre. She hadn't picked a nice out-of-town spot for us to arrive at; we appeared out of thin air in a large paved square. A giant statue of a woman with her legs crossed sat in a fountain overgrown with plants. Those who had seen us arrive stared openly. I smiled and waved, and they dashed away. No time to worry about what they thought. I turned to Olivia.

"Subtlety isn't something you understand, is it?" I hissed, but she was focusing on the ground beneath us. "Here?" I asked. I searched and found an enormous underground cavern that resembled the Liverpool and Glasgow sites, but this one was deserted.

Tina caught my arm and pointed. There were large wooden screens erected at one end of the square, pronouncing that the metro was being extended. "Maybe the building works got in the way?"

Whatever the reason, we were in the wrong place. I convinced Olivia that we should avoid too much attention and she opened the next portal behind a statue of Queen Victoria obscured by the building works, out of sight of the public.

There was no-one to see us arrive in Leeds. We had appeared in the centre of a sports field. Raked seating surrounded us, and the grass beneath our feet was close-cropped, and well tended.

"Is this a cricket pitch?" I asked.

"Headingley," Tina said. "What? I follow Yorkshire," she added.

"Hush, he's here," Olivia snapped, causing Tina and I to look around. "Underground," Olivia sighed. I probed beneath our feet again and detected another Vault. This one was not as large as the others, but more densely packed with Fae creatures than they had been.

"Is it shielded?" Tina asked. "Has he opened a portal?"

I couldn't detect either, which meant that at least we'd got here before he'd started his attack. It also meant we should have been able to make our way inside without too much trouble. My efforts to open a portal of my own, however, failed on every attempt.

"You've not really seen it, you can't visualise it well enough by remote viewing," Olivia reminded me.

"Wait, so we can't get in?" Tina asked. "OK, let's go back to the offices and use the Divide."

Olivia shook her head. "No priming agent," she said. "These sites were officially unused, so they didn't keep any handy. That was what my source told me, and I have no reason to believe he was lying." I would have to ignore these reminders of Olivia's true nature until this was over.

I bit down my retort. "What now?" I asked.

"We take a look inside," Olivia said, as if it was the simplest thing in the world. And with that, she pointed her hands at the ground beneath our feet.

A patch of grass and soil lifted, dissipating into dust as it did so. As we watched, a clump of more mud and clay followed it out, dissolving as it reached the surface. Tina shook her head and muttered about it being sacrilege to treat the pitch like this, but focused her efforts on helping. I joined in and soon a stream of earth was flowing out of the ground, clouds of dust billowing around us. It took a few minutes to reach rock, but the spell Olivia had used made short work of it, and before long we had come to a layer of red bricks which formed the roof of the Vault.

Olivia stepped up to the edge of the hole. I peered down alongside her and while perspective narrowed it to a pinprick at the bottom, I could see light down there, and cages. I wasn't sure it'd be enough to work with, but Olivia let out a giggle and opened a portal just to one side of the hole. We stepped through and emerged inside the Vault.

The view she'd had wasn't perfect. We came out of the portal a short distance above the ground and fell the rest of the way.

We picked ourselves up, and brushing off the dust we looked around. Just as in the other Vaults cages stretched as far as we could see in every direction, piled high and every one containing something dreadful. We had detected no other people here, so at least we could confront Byron and defeat him without other distractions. The attacks we used in London had been ineffective, but we had a plan. First, we had to find him. I tossed caution to the winds and sent out a searching wave of magical energy to every corner of the Vault. He'd detect us just as easily as we'd detect him, but there was little point in delaying the confrontation any further.

"He's at the back of the offices, coming this way," I informed the others, who nodded and spread out to cover as many of the aisles as possible. As soon as we were in position, Byron's unmistakable outline appeared in the doorway at the end of the Vault.

"I am very disappointed," he called out, "though not entirely surprised. Your grandfather was weak and sentimental too, and that killed him. Or more accurately, I did. He begged, of course." He was trying to goad me into striking before we were ready, anger me into making a mistake, and it was working. "Pleaded with me not to do it." I faced him along the corridor between the nightmare creatures and stood my ground. I forced myself to relax, to let the energies build.

"What happens now?" I asked. I gestured at the surrounding creatures. "You release this lot and start converting our world into another copy of yours?"

"More or less," he shrugged, pacing towards me. "These are just the start. With humanity panicked and distracted, I can open as many gateways Over There as I like, allow my fellows to aid me."

"Revealing that world to so many people would be disastrous," I said. "You've seen what it does to our minds. Do you want to rule over the insane?"

He sighed. "You still think I want to rule? I just want a home, to be with my peers instead of you pitiful wretches. My fellows will welcome a fresh world to discover, just as your forebears relished unknown lands and horizons to explore. But then, I think you understand me all too well, and are merely stalling for time as your friends try to surround me."

Time was up, I put up my shield. Shimmers in my peripheral vision told me Tina was in position at the end of the aisle to my right, while

Olivia was ready on my left. I launched the first attack straight at Byron, a stabbing jolt of electricity to the head.

As expected, he deflected it easily. Two more attacks, one fire and one ice, jetted towards him from the sides right on cue. As he swung his shield to counter them, I gestured and flung open the cages beside him, nudging the beasts inside with magical encouragement to leave their confinement. Momentarily distracted by the movements around him, Byron hesitated just for a moment... and I collapsed a section of roof above him. Bricks, rocks and earth showered down, and he reoriented his shield. The creatures on either side howled as they clawed at his defences and retreated as the debris bounced off his shield and hit them.

"Block them in!" I shouted. I focused my shield in front of me to make sure they couldn't leave the aisle, Tina and Olivia doing the same behind him. While the falling brickwork blinded Byron, I opened the remaining cages between us and shouted "now!"

We sprang our trap. We flipped our shields around and joined them together, forming them into a bubble around Byron. We trapped him inside with the beasts he'd planned to use.

We instantly realised our mistake. Byron shook the last of the earth from his shield and reabsorbed his own protective bubble. The creatures thought he was undefended and turned to attack. Before they could, he drained them of power. Some larger ones stumbled forward, but most fell where they stood, unable to withstand the draw on their life's energies. Before we could react, a circle of bizarre corpses surrounded him and he was stronger than ever. Unearthly cries and screams issued from the cages around us as the other beasts fought to escape.

"I thought you would understand, Richard," Byron shouted. "One day you will, you cannot ignore your true nature. If you live long enough."

Lances of sickly green light seared out from Byron's body, towards each of the three of us. Hurriedly, we focused our own energy on strengthening our trap and contained the assault. A few more of those would overpower us, unless we did something fast. I trusted the others to understand as I copied Byron's example and drew power from the remaining caged beasts behind me, using the stolen energy to strengthen and shrink the bubble around our enemy.

"Surrender!" I shouted. "We can work together to repair your world, return these creatures and heal the damage."

The howls and rattling of cages around us reached a crescendo as the beasts fought for their lives, but the voice of Byron overpowered them as he sensed his prison closing on him.

"I will destroy this world, starting with you three insignificant insects. An old woman, a cripple and a teacher against me? I will stand over your lifeless bodies and laugh!"

With no more surviving creatures to draw on, we'd limited his powers. I had a larger number left to drain than he had already exhausted. As we tightened the surrounding net, more and more of the surrounding beasts fell silent. I just kept pulling in the power I needed to squeeze Byron into surrender. His words changed from insults and threats to arcane words in a language we didn't understand.

He fell silent as the shell around him shrank and he slumped for-ward. His head dropped, his chin resting on his mighty chest, and his shoulders sagged. I inched forward to see better, expecting a trick. His breath was shallow, a vein in his neck pulsing rapidly.

Tina and Olivia approached as cautiously as I had. They kept their parts of the trap in place. We had to trust that our shield was enough to keep him from using the spell he had to escape London, or he would have done it as soon as he realised he was trapped and outmatched. I needed to be sure he was drained.

"I'm going to check," I told the others. "Hold him."

I opened a tiny gap no larger than a pinprick in my side of the shield. As soon as my attention was directed inside, I knew he was bluffing. Vast reserves of energy remained. Some inside his body, but most of it ricocheting around inside his cell. As fast as I realised this, I slammed shut the hole I'd made, but too late. Byron's energy had been free for a reason, bouncing around inside the bubble to probe for any weakness or opening, and I'd just given it one. It found my spy-hole, a thin tendril of magic spearing through and then widening. Like a hose filling with water it expanded, pushing my shield open around it until it was the size of a fist, an arm, and still growing.

"He's bluffing!" I shouted, but Tina and Olivia had already seen the danger. I tried to create a new protection for myself, to defend myself from Byron's probe without releasing him, but it was too hard. The stronger I made my shield, the less energy I had to spare for imprisoning him, and the harder it made it to reach the surrounding creatures. I needed their power to pump energy into the trap.

"I have to drain them!" I shouted, and pulled the very last of the energy from the imprisoned terrors around us, as much to deny Byron their power as to use it myself. I was backing away, in a stalemate with Byron for the time being. As much as he could open the hole in the bubble, if he tried to turn that energy on me, it would snap shut around him again. And I couldn't do anything without risking my hold on his prison.

"Release me!" he bellowed. "You cannot win!"

"You're wrong," Olivia shouted back. "We can drain this entire world to keep you in there, if we have to!" My stomach lurched as I realised she might try. Byron laughed. Evidently he thought she was bluffing, or at least incapable of doing it.

I could see no way to hurt him now, but he was spending his energies opening up the shield. He would run out eventually, but so would we. To avoid his overhearing our planning, I pulled the Scry from my pocket and Tina, Olivia and I started a hasty discussion.

"Just keep him in there," Olivia suggested. "You can take whatever power you need from all around us and wait for him to tire."

"No, it's too risky, draining that much power," Tina said. "If we just squeeze him tighter, he'll have to use up his energies just to resist us."

"OK, let's try that," I agreed. But Byron had no trouble preventing the bubble from contracting further.

"OK. Desperate times call for desperate measures," I said, and outlined my idea. Olivia thought it might work, but Tina was horrified.

"You can't," she cried out loud. "It's suicide!" Byron spun to regard her, a quizzical look on his face. That wasn't the distraction I'd expected, but it was just what I required. Without further debate, I opened a portal beneath his feet.

Chapter Thirty-Nine

A Horrifying Glimpse

I planned to let him drop through the opening I'd created and reappear miles above the earth. If we maintained our prison-like bubble, he'd not be able to levitate against the ground, or create a portal to escape. The ground beneath my feet softened as the portal began expanding, and I hoped I'd be able to stop its growth before it swallowed us.

That's when I noticed Olivia's chanting. Whatever she was attempting to do, I didn't recognise the spell, nor could I properly sense the shape of it. This was something new, something different.

Something from Over There.

I looked into the opening void beneath me, the countryside distant as if from an aircraft window, but then the view swam in front of my eyes and became indistinct and blurred as if I'd been drinking.

"Look away!" came Tina's shout. The beasts were silent now, but something dulled our hearing.

The view flickered, replacing English country fields with something darker for an instant, as if I'd blinked and seen an after-image of a bright light.

"Don't look!" Tina shouted once more, but I didn't need telling again. That glimpse of whatever it had been was enough. I tore my eyes away. Tina was holding Byron in place with increasing difficulty as her strength faltered, and Olivia focused her energies on whatever she was doing. I reinforced Tina's spell, and Byron struggled harder as the door beneath him opened wider.

Tina and I stepped back as we felt the hole widen. My eyes were dragged back to the scene below. This time the flicker lasted more than a blink, and the outlines of buildings burned into my vision. They looked organic, as if grown rather than built. I forced myself to look away again, to see Olivia straining hard against the spell she was casting.

"Do you need help?" I called out to her, but she didn't answer, just kept chanting her strange sounds as the tendons in her neck stood out with the effort.

"What is it?" I shouted to Tina. She shook her head, though whether she didn't know or just didn't want to say wasn't clear.

"It is my old home," Byron said. "Over There, as you call it. I shall not go." Byron protested. "I told you it was no longer a home for me and I meant it, your world has corrupted it too much. It would be kinder to kill me." The view beneath us flickered again, and I thought he might be right.

"We can't go through," I called to Olivia, "we'd never survive either."

"You didn't care about that when you wanted to drop him from a cloud," Tina called back to me. "But he's right, this is not a better solution." Olivia ignored us. The view through the portal was changing, more often showing the other realm than our own, and I was finding it harder to avoid staring.

There were creatures like the ones now dead in the surrounding cages, living and moving around freely. There were some I didn't recognise, some familiar and some stranger still, all unaware of our presence. I prayed it would stay that way and stepped back again.

Byron shifted his attention to Olivia, trying to drain her power and close the portal, but she blocked him. His efforts to escape redoubled, but he had nothing to draw energy from within his prison. Tina and I were holding him now, even without Olivia's help. She looked ready to pass out from the exertion. Byron's protests became more and more guttural, and he was once again the other-worldly beast I'd forgotten he was.

Was he going insane at the sight of his former home? Or was it just fury at his defeat? Why couldn't we just kill him? Why did Olivia want to send him back Over There instead? I would ask her when this was over, assuming the effort didn't kill her first. She looked older, the magic extracting its price.

The flickering beneath us stopped. An irresistible curiosity drew my eyes back downwards.

I screamed.

Even now, I barely believe what I saw. The view Over There has affected my mind in ways I'm still learning to understand, and I doubt the evidence of my senses.

From what Tina told me afterwards, I'd held on to the spell surrounding Byron despite my shock, and she'd managed not to peek into the abyss. Olivia had stabilised the portal enough to be safe to traverse, if anything to do with that place could be considered safe, and pushed him through.

She sent him over, back to the strange land he'd once called home. I remember his screams, the rending of his soul. Tina tells me I tried to jump in after him, convulsed with grief and guilt and who knows what else, but Olivia had exerted her will and pushed me back from the edge. I had a cracked rib and a flowering bruise across my side to show for it, but Tina assured me it was a lucky escape.

"She kept us away from the threshold," Tina explained. "As soon as Byron passed through, our containment spells stopped working. Something to do with the portal maybe, or our variety of magic can't work Over There, I'm not sure."

"What does Olivia say?" I asked. Another memory surfaced, and Tina confirmed what I thought I knew.

"She went in with him. I doubt she wanted to risk his escaping back over here again, but it wouldn't have mattered, he just pulled her in. As soon as she passed through, the portal flickered back to our world once more and collapsed."

"It's over?" I said. I looked around us at the cages full of creatures now decaying without their life force.

"For now," Tina replied.

Chapter Forty

An Uneasy Calm

We lacked the magical strength to go back to London the quick way, so we took a slow train from Leeds Station. Images from our battle flashed before my eyes whenever I blinked, and every squeal of the train's brakes made me jump. Some aspect of the sound recalled Byron's scream, reached into my brain and dragged me back there. At one point, a child threw a tantrum a few seats over and I had to press my hands over my ears to block it out, closing my eyes until the afterimages forced them open again.

Tina tried to distract me, brought me tea and something to eat. I ate mechanically, taking no pleasure from the act. The tea burned my mouth, but I felt nothing. Every attempt she made to engage me in conversation failed. Nothing mattered, not now I'd learned the truth of our shallow existence. There was another world. Another universe out there, so strange and terrifying that it made this one look as inconsequential as tissue paper and about as safe. And had Byron been telling the truth? Was a part of me a part of that world too? I wanted to sleep, but dared not close my eyes. I wanted to run, but had nowhere to go. I wanted to turn back the clock and have had nothing to do with this infernal Society.

Tina continued talking, wondering how to tell who to trust now, whether we'd still have to face Green's allies, or whether they had been exposed and dealt with already. I tried to focus, to listen to her ideas and offer some of my own, but my mind raced and my heart pounded in my ears. Then she said something which broke through.

"At least they won't be as tough as Byron."

I nodded at Tina and tried to smile. She rested her hand on my shoulder, within moments my eyes closed, and I slept.

I awoke at King's Cross as everyone around us started preparing to leave the train. We made our way through the crowds at the station to find a quiet spot. Tina had recovered enough power to open a doorway to the Divide. As we slipped through, I saw a small child in a Harry Potter scarf tug frantically on his oblivious mother's arm to tell her he had seen real wizards.

Back at the Society, we faced scenes of chaos. Dozens of wounded were lying on blankets on the floor of the reception area, being tended to by the Healers. More blankets covered figures who hadn't survived. There were more of the latter.

When we exited the Divide we were besieged with questions. I retreated into panic and fear again, but Tina seized control.

"Who's in charge?" she shouted. Silence fell for a moment before Mr Red pushed through the crowd. He'd changed his suit and shirt since we'd last seen him, but had yet to put on a tie.

"I am," he replied.

"And where is your loyalty?" Tina asked. Gasps from the onlookers greeted this display of confidence.

"To humanity," Red answered. "And those who protect it."

"Good enough for me," I said. "As long as you're not one of Green's men, we're on the same side."

"Far from it," he said. "But let us take this conversation somewhere more private."

He led us along the corridor to his office. Sitting behind his desk, he steepled his fingers.

"So," he began, and then stopped. With a heavy sigh, he sat back, exhausted. There was a knock on the door, then Marlin appeared, pushing a tea trolley into the room.

I breathed a sigh of relief. "Thank goodness you're OK, Marlin. I hate that we got you caught up in all of this."

Marlin pushed a plateful of chocolate covered biscuits at me, and I took one. "It was my decision to assist you," he said. "And I am glad you're alive. I've finished watching all those movies you got me already, and could use some more." He grinned and patted my hand before leaving.

Red added, "He was very helpful at filling us in on some of your activities. Something you might have done yourselves, I might add."

"We didn't know who we could trust," Tina explained. "I'm sorry."

Red issued a sound which might have been a grunt of agreement or annoyance. "Why don't you fill me in now," he said. "Unless you still think I'm part of the whole evil scheme, that is?"

"Green and Byron," I said. "They were behind it all. Green thought he was getting a chance to seize power, releasing Fae into the world only to ride to the rescue, but he was played by Byron all along. *He* just wanted a new home."

"And revenge," Tina added. Red nodded.

We started to explain. The Vaults spread around the country, the stockpiled beasts ready and primed to attack, the experiments and exploitation that had been going on despite a surface of respectability being enforced. Not one revelation surprised him.

"Olivia helped us," I said, staring him in the eyes. This time I was rewarded with a slight flinch, and would have smiled at having landed a blow if I hadn't remembered Mrs Orange. "I'm sorry," I added, "but we wouldn't have won without her help."

He contained his fury with more self-control than I could have managed under similar circumstances. I just wished he'd say something.

"You won't have to worry about her any more, though," Tina said. "She went Over There again, with Byron." She looked over at me for a moment and then added, "They're probably both dead by now."

Red raised an eyebrow at this, but still didn't speak. We sat in silence for a moment.

"So you weren't part of it," I said, hoping it sounded more like a statement than the question I was really asking.

There was an interminable pause before he replied. "A few of us knew about Green, for a while."

"And you did nothing?" The words were out before I could stop them. He regarded me severely.

"Nothing overt, no. We appreciated he had allies, but we were unsure if they had the same agenda as he did. Something you discovered for yourselves. And much as you did, we had trouble identifying who was trustworthy. You, for example." He pointed at me. "You were on our radar as one of Green's fellows, your friendship with Byron meant that there was no way we could trust you. And you," he pointed at Tina, "were tarred with the same brush. We knew about your training sessions and research trips, so you were a suspect too."

"I had to play the part to find out what they were up to!" I said.

"We considered that possibility," Red said, "but you kept up the pretence so well we were preparing to take you down along with Green."

"What stopped you?" Tina asked.

"Marlin. You didn't fool him, at least. He's been a significant help to us throughout, since he can go anywhere and no-one gives him a second glance. Most of our knowledge came from his surveillance and eavesdropping."

"But we didn't speak about this in front of him," I pointed out. "Or anyone, so how did he know which side we were on?"

"Who do you think slipped you the memo detailing the worst of the Society's excesses?" Red said. "And who do you think handled your requests for more of the documents? He could tell by your reactions where your conscience lay. And he took a shine to you. Most people treat him like a servant or worse, so your kinder treatment might have swayed his opinion. He was very fond of your grandfather for the same reason."

I swallowed hard.

"And Green's allies, where are they now?" Tina asked.

"Mostly dead," Red stated. "Some in hiding, some imprisoned. We were fortunate that Green fell as soon as he did. His human allies panicked when they realised what Byron had planned. Apparently it was fine to massacre countless innocents in the pursuit of power, but if they would get nothing out of it, they didn't want blood on their hands."

"And the non-human ones?" I asked.

"They're the mostly dead ones," Red said. "Those who wanted to fight. They believed Byron would prevail and build their promised land on the ruins of ours. He had a poetic turn of phrase, rather like his namesake. I'm pleasantly surprised that he has failed."

"You didn't think we could win?" Tina gasped.

"Would you have bet against him?" Red replied.

"What was your plan?" I asked. "I'd hate to think we deprived you of your chance to shine."

"Oh, it was broadly the same as yours," he replied. "Give Green enough rope to hang himself with, step in and stop him. Our force was on the way to his office when you stormed in there, trashed the place and disappeared, and we had no way to follow you. Your trick of knocking the Vaults off the Divide network caused us a few problems, too. And your showdown took place off the grid, as it were."

"You had a plan for Byron?" I asked.

Red nodded. "Kill or be killed. We didn't know he was plotting against Green, I admit, but it didn't make much difference at the end of the day. They both had to be stopped. Congratulations you two, you did it."

"So it's over?" Tina asked.

"If Byron is dead or trapped Over There, if Olivia is likewise, if we have rooted out all of their conspirators, if all of a dozen things come out in our favour then yes, we are safe. But I think you would agree we would be foolish to trust to luck."

"What comes next?" I asked. "If Green and Byron were collecting all those creatures for so long, there must be even more weak spots than before. You're going to be busier than ever."

"Indeed we are," Red agreed. "This Society still stands and has a duty to protect humanity from the Fae threat. You have performed that duty admirably, both of you, and there will always be a place for you here."

"It'd better be a nicer place than you've kept me in so far," Tina said. "My lab needs an upgrade, and I could use some help…"

Red laughed. "Ms Black, my predecessor may have underestimated you, but I will not be making the same mistake. It occurs to me that there is a position recently vacated by Byron, in directing the magical research for the Society."

Tina stuttered for a moment. "You'd better not be expecting me to continue his horrible experiments," she said. "I'm not like him."

"Which is exactly why you will be ideal for the role," Red replied. "I said you would direct our research and I stand by that. Whatever you feel is the correct approach will be up to you. Although I regret there will be more oversight than the previous team experienced. You understand, we can't have rogue elements pursuing their own agendas any longer."

"I don't know what to say," Tina said. "Thank you! I won't let you down!" She beamed with delight. "I have some ideas already, based on what Richard has discovered. We can probe how it is he's able to sense the shape of a spell just by observing it, and…"

Red held up his hands in mock surrender. "All in good time, Ms Black. Thanks to your escapades it will take us a little while to return the laboratories to working order. And I think you could both do with a rest, hmm?" Tina stood, but I made no move to leave. Tina's words had reminded me. "Was there something else?"

"Byron told me something," I said. "He said that my ancestry might be a part of why I can do magic."

"You think there is a Fae in your family tree?" Red smiled. "It's more than likely. Oh, don't worry, we've known for many years that magic runs in families, that it has a lot to do with blood lines. That sort of thing used to happen all the time, centuries ago. Chances are more than half the population has a fairy relative somewhere in their past."

"He said my genuine nature would come out, that I'd…"

"Nonsense, he was just trying to upset you. You're probably more closely related to the Royal Family than the Fae! Try not to worry." He smiled, not altogether reassuringly. "What day is it today?"

I checked my watch. "Thursday."

"Then I shall see you both bright and early on Monday morning."

EPILOGUE

I was running. I couldn't tell you what I was searching for, what I was fleeing or where I was heading. I couldn't even have told you where I was. An adversary pursued me unseen along unfamiliar corridors lined with entrances that were never the one I sought. I charged past identical doors, terrified to look behind me in case I glimpsed my pursuer. Corners turned the wrong way. Walls loomed overhead one moment only to retreat to infinity the next. Windows showed me views of London aflame, then snatches of that disturbing landscape I'd glimpsed through Olivia's portal.

Strange noises surrounded me. Growls, the scrape of claws on stone, half-recognised voices calling to me or urging me to stay away. I ran, my feet stumbling and my breath catching in my throat for hours...

I woke with a start. The train rattled through rainy countryside on the way to Bristol.

"The nightmare again?" Tina asked. I nodded.

"I still can't see who it is," I said. "I feel like if I knew…"

"It's your mind trying to make sense of everything," Tina reassured me. "There's no deeper meaning, no message from her. Or him, come to that."

"I know," I said, and took a sip of my now lukewarm coffee. The dream had faded as it always did, leaving a tantalising sense of meaning lost. Tina was right — it wasn't a message, just the random firings of a brain stretched to breaking point. The past month had given few opportunities to rest. We'd purged the last of Green's supporters from the Society and made a start on repairing the damage caused by his and Byron's collecting trips.

The Society had lost a great number of members, and the number of weak spots around the country was overwhelming. I'd come up with a spell to locate the worst of them, similar to the one I'd used to uncover the Vaults. Blobs of wax dotted every map so densely as to obscure many of the place names. Even with careful prioritisation of the largest breaches we were dreadfully exposed, and we had work for months more just to get back to a state of relative safety. This was not to mention the risk of any of Green's or Byron's supporters still being at large.

Red had confined me to the offices most of the time. He explained that I was most useful there coordinating the repair works, sending out the teams to seal the breaches and deal with the creatures that had come through. I had my suspicions he was concerned for my sanity after glimpsing Over There and was keeping me out of the way as much as possible. With difficulty I'd finally convinced him to let Tina and I investigate what had been reported as wild animal attacks in the West Country.

The train rolled into Reading station. Still an hour to go. I picked up the newspaper to distract myself with the crossword and a plain white envelope fell from the pages. Tina and I stared at it for a moment, then looked around to see who might have left it. I glimpsed a short, elderly woman on the platform, her grey hair trying to escape a bun, before she vanished into the crowd.

I tipped up the envelope and regarded the black card with the intricate silver sigil embossed in foil.

Can You Help Me Out?

Thank you so much for reading this book, and I'd love to know what you thought of it.

Reviews are vital for an author, not just so we can find out what people think, but because it also helps more readers like you find the books they're going to love. So please do consider leaving a review on Amazon.

If you're not sure how, it's very simple:

Click here to leave a review!

Learn the secrets of the Fae Defence Society

Visit the website and sign up to receive a secret bundle of files revealing the work of the Fae Defence Society going on throughout history. This will also sign you up to our mailing list to keep you updated with the fight against the fae.

https://faedefencesociety.com/newsletter/
Stay watchful.

Also By Mark Hood

War of the Worlds Sequel Series

Amy's Journal (website exclusive)
The Return of the Martians
Earth Under the Martians - Coming soon!

Fae Defence Society Series

Jacob's War
The Fairies Want Me Dead

Tales from the Treehouse Anthologies

A is for Apple - contains my short story Skin Deep
B is for Beauty - contains my short story West of the Moon

ACKNOWLEDGMENTS

Special thanks to the first people who read this novel, in various states of incompleteness. Julian Barr, Kerrie Oman, Barb Reimer: it's changed a lot since you first encouraged me, entirely down to your comments. Ian Sainsbury, you went above & beyond to support a first-time author, for which I will always be grateful. Your advice force me to make some difficult choices, but the book is stronger because of all of you.

Mark Stay: you gave me a boost when I needed it, and reassured me that this story didn't belong in the drawer. Any hyphens left in the manuscript now are there on purpose, and not just to annoy you – except that one.

The Bestseller Academy and the BXP group were instrumental in the development and writing of this novel, and my growth as an author. I couldn't ask for a more supportive and helpful bunch of people. The sub-set of those folks who went on to form our critique team and study group are without compare. Thank you all.

Martyne, you've had faith in this story and my ability to tell it since I told you my initial idea. I hope it lives up to your belief in me.

And there will be someone I've inevitably forgotten, and a vast army of those whose tiny interactions kept me motivated. Thank you.

And thanks to you too, reader, for taking a chance on this book.